PRAISE FOR THE RED ROCK CANYON MYSTERIES

"Exciting, dense with literary references, and definitely worth a try. Legault's complex new series will appeal to conspiracy buffs, outdoors enthusiasts, and literary detectives." —*Library Journal*

"A perfect recipe for conflict: big n   tive rights and history, all resulting in m   rks a series worth investing your time i

"Legault does a masterful job of making it all so believable. The human landscape in *The Slickrock Paradox* is littered with characters that are not what they seem to be, such that even the good guys are suspect, right up until the end." —*Rocky Mountain Outlook*

PRAISE FOR THE DURRANT WALLACE MYSTERIES

"Stephen Legault has proven himself to be one of the most versatile writers currently working in Canadian crime fiction." —*National Post*

"For those looking for a glint of Canadian history set in a riveting narrative, Canmore writer Stephen Legault's *The End of the Line* combines the guilty pleasure of a page-turning murder mystery with the brain food found in Pierre Berton's history books." —*Avenue Magazine*

PRAISE FOR THE COLE BLACKWATER MYSTERIES

"The Cole Blackwater stories are among the most riveting today, and *The Vanishing Track* is the best yet in this intensely dramatic series." —*Hamilton Spectator*

THE

SAME

3: THE RED ROCK CANYON MYSTERIES

RIVER TWICE

Stephen Legault

TouchWood
Editions

TouchWood Editions
touchwoodeditions.com

LIBRARY AND ARCHIVES CANADA CATALOGUING IN PUBLICATION
Legault, Stephen, 1971–, author
The same river twice / Stephen Legault.

(The Red Rock Canyon mysteries ; 3)
Issued in print and electronic formats.
ISBN 978-1-77151-117-9

I. Title. II. Series: Legault, Stephen, 1971– . Red Rock Canyon mysteries ; 3.

PS8623.E46633S24 2015   C813'.6   C2015-904117-1

Editor: Frances Thorsen
Design: Pete Kohut
Cover image: Stephen Legault
Author photo: Dan Anthon

We gratefully acknowledge the financial support for our publishing activities from the Government of Canada through the Canada Book Fund and the Canada Council for the Arts, and from the Province of British Columbia through the British Columbia Arts Council and the Book Publishing Tax Credit.

The interior pages of this book have been printed on 100% post-consumer recycled paper, processed chlorine free, and printed with vegetable-based inks.

1 2 3 4 5   19 18 17 16 15

PRINTED IN CANADA

For the Colorado River and all
who love and fight to defend it

THEY WALKED FROM THE FIERCE heat into a startling coolness. The only colors left in the world seemed to be the raw burnt umber of the cliffs that jutted from the sandy wash and the dazzling blue of the sky wedged between them. The only sound left in the world was the beating of wings: a blue-black raven cutting the stillness with its heavy flapping. The only scent left was the heady perfume of desert evening primrose, lingering in the morning stillness.

Silas Pearson led the way, moving back and forth along the narrow canyon's bottom, searching under overhanging rocks, in clumps of salt brush, and in tangles of juniper branches suspended from previous flash floods. Robbie Pearson, his face shielded by a broad-brimmed hat, his eyes shielded by sunglasses, followed, searching the alcoves that his father bypassed. "This place have a name?" he asked, his voice small in the emptiness.

"Horse Canyon," said Silas.

"Everything around here seems to be named Horse."

"Most folks around here like horses more than people."

They rounded another bend in the canyon, the walls reaching five hundred feet above them, the sky a narrow sliver hedged between varnish-stained walls. The black streaks, a mixture of clay, iron, and manganese oxide, created alternating patterns of bright red with near black. It made the canyon walls appear articulated.

"You smell that?" asked Silas.

"Nope."

"Water."

The canyon floor was as dry as talcum, the red sand ninety degrees where the sun shone on it. They turned a corner and there it was, at the base of an unscalable overhang: a pool of rust-colored water twenty feet across. A little brown bat darted from one shadow to the next. Silas walked past the pool and into the deep recess in the stone behind it. He searched through the jumble of logs wedged there and, finding nothing, sat down in the stillness. The overhang extended ten feet above him and was thirty feet in height.

"What's up there?"

"More canyon. It reaches back another fifteen or twenty miles into the Maze."

"What's the Maze?"

"Edward Abbey called it *Terra Incognito*. *I* wouldn't go that far. It's part of Canyonlands National Park. It's accessible only by a rough Jeep trail. Fifty years ago it was one of the most remote places in the United States. Today it's more popular. It's still pretty rough country, but anybody with a good four-wheel drive and a few dozen gallons of water can drive in and camp and explore."

"Have you searched there?"

"I've been in twice, both times just to get my bearings, hike out a few of the most common routes."

"Can we get up this overhang?" Robbie tilted his head back so he was looking straight up at the pour-off. His hat fell off into the pool behind him. Silas laughed.

"You'd better get that before it sinks to the bottom."

Robbie fished his hat out of the gloomy brown water. He wrung it out and held it in his hand. "Can we get up?"

"No. But there's another way. We can go up Water Canyon and over Shot Canyon and come at it from Standing Rock. It will be a haul, but we can do it. We might take our packs and make a few days out of it."

Robbie just nodded, put his hat on his head, and started back down the narrow grotto. Silas watched him go, admiring his son's long stride and lean frame. Silas lingered in the cool of the shade for a few more minutes and then followed Robbie to the Green River.

LEE'S FERRY, SIX months earlier: he dreamt. She was floating, face down, her dress blooming around her like filigree. The water was as red as the sandstone cliffs that rose up from the river, almost still. She was drifting downstream. Silas stood on the shore, up to his knees in the water, feeling the pull of the current. He watched her glide toward him, bile rising in his mouth, fear coating his throat with something black and raw. When she was close to him he pushed into the current, the water eclipsing his thighs, then his waist. He felt it tug at him, and in the dream he wanted nothing more than to float away with her.

She was in his arms then, the white dress wrapping itself around him like the tentacles of some leviathan. The water was the color of tomato soup and surged around them. Penelope turned over in his arms. Her face, ghostly white and starkly contrasted against the red river, was waxy and drawn tight against her narrow bones. Without opening her eyes she spoke:

"All is in flux," Silas heard, "as Heraclites thought."

Was this another Edward Abbey quote? wondered Silas.

The water surged and he felt his grip failing. Then she was gone, slipping from his arms, down the river, around the bend in the canyon.

THE CASTLE VALLEY, the month before: his son Robbie had arrived for a visit. Silas stood before his maps, a pile of books on the small table in the living room. Each was a dog-eared, dust-caked copy of an

Edward Abbey volume. Silas contemplated the floor-to-ceiling topographic sheets, his finger tracing different canyons as they threaded their way across the Island in the Sky, or through the Maze, and down into the Green River.

"Have you ever used this stove, Dad?" Robbie called from the kitchen.

"Yeah, of course," Silas answered without taking his finger from the map.

"You don't have any cooking oil."

"I think there's some in with my camping gear." Silas picked up one of the books and read the table of contents. "What do you know about Heraclites?" he called toward the kitchen. The sound of sizzling oil could be heard.

"Not much. He's famous for a line about stepping twice into the same river."

"That's right. Heraclites said, 'You cannot step twice into the same river, because other waters are constantly moving on.'"

"That sounds right. Why?" Robbie's head appeared at the doorway to the kitchen.

"I can't find the sentence *All is in flux as Heraclites thought* in any of Abbey's books." Silas had told his son about his last dream about Penelope. "But I wonder . . ." continued Silas. Robbie stood watching his father. Silas held up a paperback edition of *Down the River*, one of Abbey's collections of essays, published after *Desert Solitaire*. "I wonder if what she means is to search in a place where Abbey wrote about the same river twice."

"Where is that?"

"In this book Abbey writes an essay called *Down the River with Major Powell*, and then a piece called *Down the River with Henry David Thoreau*. Both are set on the Green River. The same river twice."

"What do you want to do?" Robbie was back in the kitchen.

"Go down the river."

THE DAYS TURNED to weeks. They measured time by sunrise and sunset. They made camp, searched for a few hours or a day, slept under the canopy of cottonwoods and starlight, and put the canoe back into the water again. They prowled among the pictographs and granaries of the ancient Pueblo people and walked desert bighorn trails along perilous cliff faces and into box canyons where fresh cougar scat glistened in the blazing sun.

There was nothing to see. She was nowhere to be found.

After nearly four weeks they came to Water Canyon, a broad cleft in the sandstone walls just a few miles from where the Green River met the Colorado.

In the morning they shouldered backpacks and, leaving the canoe tied to a heavy clump of tamarisk on the beach, started to hike up the canyon. They stopped often to search among the jumble of boulders in the canyon floor. There was water along much of their route and they refilled their canteens often. At sundown they sat in the shadow of Chimney Rock, looking out over the Maze.

"You think she's in *there*?" asked Robbie.

"I have no idea where she is."

THREE DAYS LATER, sunburnt, exhausted, and out of food, they crossed the slickrock divide between Shot and Water Canyons, sky-lighting the cairns so they could navigate the drop-off in Water Canyon by moonlight. Two hours later, their feet bloody with blisters, they were on the narrow trail above their camp on the Green River.

"What is *that*?" asked Robbie, pointing toward the shore where in the darkness their canoe was tied. They could see a red glow against the sandstone cliffs.

"I don't know . . . but I think it's a fire."

They rushed down the track, fearful that the tamarisk had somehow been set ablaze and their boat would be lost. Instead of brush fire, what they saw on the shore was a campfire, four people silhouetted by its light. A heavy aluminum powerboat was anchored against the sand. Silas could see its hull reflecting the light of the flames. He made out the National Park Service insignia on its side.

"What's going on?" Robbie spoke quietly, almost in a whisper.

Silas said nothing. He walked through the tamarisk and emerged on the sandy beach. He dropped his pack.

"Silas, that you?"

"Who's that?"

"It's Stan Baton, Silas." The Chief Park Ranger for Canyonlands and Arches National Parks.

"And Special Agent Eugene Nielsen, Dr. Pearson."

"If you guys came all the way down here to lock me up, you'd better have brought some beer."

"Silas, we're not here to arrest you," said Stan. Silas watched his face by the light of the fire. "You want to have a seat here on the rocks? We've got some news to tell you."

Silas felt the hair on the back of his neck stand on end. "What is it, Stan?"

"You wanna sit?"

"No. What is it?"

"It's Penelope, Silas. We've found her. We found her body, that is."

SILAS PEARSON HAD NEVER GIVEN up. He had come close. More times than he could count he had come to some precipice, some box canyon, some bureaucratic wall. He'd considered surrendering, but he hadn't.

"Where is she, Stan?"

"Sit down, Silas. Let's talk. Robbie, grab a seat; maybe your dad will too."

"Come on, Dad, let's sit."

"I don't want to sit. Where is she, Stan?"

"Her body was found in Lake Powell."

"You're kidding me."

"No, I wish I was. We found her in Glen Canyon, at the bottom of the Hole in the Rock."

"What is that?" Robbie stood next to his father.

Stan answered: "It's a man-made ramp, a passageway, that drops a thousand feet from the canyon rim down to the River. The Mormons chiselled it out of the sandstone in 1880 in order to get across the Colorado. Most of it got flooded when they built Glen Canyon Dam . . ."

Silas shook his head. "Stan, when . . . what, I—?"

"Silas, you look like you're going to fall over. Sit down. John," Stan said to one of the other men, "why don't you get Dr. Pearson a beer. There's a few in the cooler. And bring him and Robbie those sandwiches we picked up."

"This is John Danforth, the sheriff of Kane County. They are sharing jurisdiction with the feds on this. And you remember Tom, my Special Investigator. I'll tell you everything I can, Silas. Penelope's body was found about a week ago by a—"

"And you're just telling me now?"

"We didn't know it was her, Dr. Pearson," said Eugene Nielsen. Silas looked at him through the flames. "We needed to identify the body before we could alert you. And then we had to find you."

Baton continued. "She was found by a party of houseboaters who were on Lake Powell. They were hiking up the Hole in the Rock. The water's been dropping pretty steady this fall, and it's at its lowest since the dam was built. It appears as if her body floated up into some logs and then decomposed there. Then the water dropped. The houseboaters found her that way just above the waterline."

"Stan—"

"She was skeletal, Silas. That's all that was left. She had likely been in the water this whole time, or most of it."

"Where is she now?"

"Dr. Rain has her back in Salt Lake City. She's doing some work with her," said Nielsen.

"What work?"

"We still need to determine the cause of death. We're running a full battery of tests."

"Was she murdered, Stan?"

Before Nielsen could cut him off, Stan answered. "Yes, Silas. She was."

AT NINE O'CLOCK IN THE morning, the jet boat cut across the surface of the Colorado River, the cliffs racing past at thirty miles an hour. Silas huddled in the front seat of the boat wearing a heavy fleece coat, a life jacket, and a wool cap. He craned his neck to look behind him. Stan Baton piloted the boat; Robbie stood next to him. The two men yelled over the growl of the engine. The other three law enforcement officers sat quietly, watching the cliffs, the sky, and him.

Silas caught one last glimpse as the Colorado disappeared beyond its confluence with the Green and into Cataract Canyon; beyond that were the drowned depths of Glen Canyon.

"THAT HAD BETTER not be a smile on your face, Agent Taylor."

"I would have thought you knew me better than that, Dr. Pearson. I'm sorry for your loss."

Silas walked up the boat ramp near Potash and set an armload of gear down next to his Outback. Robbie did the same and then returned to the boat to make another trip.

"Why don't you let your son hump your gear? You and I need to talk."

Silas looked around as if searching for any excuse to avoid this conversation but, failing to find one, simply nodded. They made their way to the shade of a cottonwood and sat down at a picnic table. Agent Nielsen joined them.

"So, Dr. Pearson, what can you tell us about your wife's death?"

Silas looked up, his eyes red from the sun and the wind. He screwed his face into a question and scratched his gray beard, full now from a month on the river. "That was going to be my question."

"This is just routine—" started Nielsen.

"There's nothing *routine* about it." Silas pursed his lips; they were dry and cracked. "I had nothing to do with Penelope's disappearance and I had nothing to do with her death. The faster you get that through your heads, the sooner we can get on to finding out who really killed her."

The three men sat in the stillness under the cottonwood. Taylor cleared his throat. "We need to establish time of death. It's going to be very difficult given the circumstances. We have your missing person's report as a starting point. Dr. Rain will give us more to go on soon. I don't want to start jumping to conclusions, Dr. Pearson, but I want to look at the possibility that the death of your wife is connected to a few other cases we're working on."

"Darcy McFarland and Kiel Pearce."

"You led us to both of those bodies. Darcy McFarland's murder last summer and Kiel Pearce's murder in the spring are both open, unsolved. We know that both Ms. McFarland and Mr. Pearce were friends with your wife."

"I think Kiel was more of an acquaintance of my wife, but I can't be certain. Penny had a lot of friends connected with her environmental advocacy that I didn't know."

"We have our own profile of the crimes that suggests those two murders are related. The nature of both crimes gives us reason to suspect that the victims knew their killer." Taylor watched Silas.

"What was the work connection between these three people?" asked Nielsen.

Silas looked over his shoulder at the jet boat and the river beyond it. "*That* was the connection. The Colorado River."

"TRISH, IT'S SILAS."

"Is it true?"

"Yes, it's true. They found Penny about a week ago. Robbie and I were on the Green River. We just got the news yesterday."

"Where are you now?"

"We're at home. We've got to come into town tomorrow morning for another friendly chat with the FBI, but I thought I'd call and tell you."

"Silas, are you okay?"

"I am. I swing back and forth. It's a good thing I don't have any furniture, because sometimes I just want to break something. But the next moment I'm serene."

"When Ken died in the spring I wanted to kill *him*."

"It's still pretty raw, I know. I'm sorry."

"There's nothing for you to be sorry about. He lived life the way he wanted to. It caught up to him."

"I miss him, Trish."

"Me too, Silas. Come by and say hello if you're in town tomorrow."

"I will."

SILAS SAT ON the edge of his bed, surrounded by topographic maps. The small lamp on the bedside table cast a yellow glow on the framed photograph in his hands. He touched the glass over the cheek of the woman immortalized there as if brushing away a tear.

He put the photo down, turned out the light, and lay on top of the sheets, staring at the ceiling. Darcy, Kiel, and Penelope: all three bodies were found along the Colorado River. All three were advocates for the watercourse. Someone, or some people, wanted all three dead, and the river was at the heart of this mystery.

4

"DR. RAIN HAS JOINED US for our conversation, Dr. Pearson."
Dwight Taylor met Silas at the front door of the Grand County
municipal building. "She wanted to share her findings with you
in person."

Silas and Robbie stepped into the building and followed the
towering black man to the familiar conference room. "You met John
from Kane County, and of course you know Grand County Sheriff
Dexter Willis. Stan Baton is representing the Park Service. As you
found out last year while we were looking into the death of the Hopi
girl, Utah is a bit of an anomaly; anywhere else, we feds would have
sole jurisdiction over a body found in a national park, monument,
or national recreation area, but here in the Beehive State we have
concurrent jurisdiction, hence the cramped seating."

Rain stood and shook Silas's hand. She smiled at him and said,
"I'm so sorry, Silas." Then she introduced herself to Robbie.

"I've heard a lot about you," Robbie said, sitting down next to
his father.

"And I've heard a lot about you."

"Alright, now that all of that is out of the way, Dr. Rain?"

Rain opened a folder, but she didn't look at any of the notes there. "I'm just going to deliver this to you straight, Silas. If you want me to stop, say so." Silas nodded and Katie continued. "Penelope de Silva, female, thirty-six years old at time of death. We identified Ms. de Silva by dental records we had on file. It is going to be difficult to be precise regarding the date of death, but I have no reason to believe that she wasn't killed right around the time you reported her missing.

"I have concluded that the cause of death was a single gunshot wound to the head. The bullet entered the frontal lobe and exited the occipital lobe. The weapon used was a large-caliber firearm, likely a pistol, and probably .44 or .45. There is some indication of a spider-web pattern around the entrance wound. This is consistent with the weapon being fired at point-blank range. There was no skin from which to take gunshot residue samples, nor could we check for powder burns as the remains had been submerged in water for too long." Katie looked at Silas.

He nodded and she continued. "The exit wound was large, and I have calculated the angle of the gunshot at about thirty-one degrees, meaning the shooter was above the victim, shooting down. There were no ballistics recovered from the body, and John Huston, our crime scene analyst, says that nothing has been recovered from the immediate vicinity of where the body was found.

"We believe that shortly after death, she was put into the water. Decomposition was slow; the water temperature was usually around forty degrees. The body may have been exposed to open air sometime in the last two years. The bones we have recovered were dry. We're working with the Park Service to gauge exactly where the water level in Lake Powell was at the time Penelope disappeared.

"We have traces of anipocere; this is a waxy, almost soapy material that is often associated with bodies recovered from water, and it helps hold tissue and bones together. Once anipocere forms it's there for good. There was some insect activity that impacted the amount, but its presence clearly shows that she was submerged for a long time. Unfortunately, we haven't been able to recover all of Ms. de Silva's bones. About seventy percent are accounted for. The recovery team is still searching the area.

"She was found entangled in logs and other driftwood material, and there was a lot of sand and silt with the skeletal remains. If she hadn't been lodged in this debris, we might never have found her. They formed something of an anchor to hold her in place and to keep her remains from dispersing.

"The only other thing I have right now is that the definitive cause of death would lead me to conclude that she died instantly. She didn't suffer."

The room was completely silent. Silas rubbed his hands together and then rubbed his face. Robbie touched his father's arm but Silas just stared at Katie Rain.

"If you have any questions I could try and answer them."

Silas started to speak but his voice was hoarse.

Dexter Willis stood. "I'll get you some water."

Silas nodded and waited. Robbie just held onto his arm.

"Here you go, Silas." Dexter put a glass of water down and Silas drank from it.

He cleared his throat. "Was anything else found around the body?"

"You mean like clothing, or jewelry?" asked Agent Taylor. "No, nothing. So long in the water means that any clothing would have decomposed, or floated away. We haven't recovered anything else from the scene. If she was wearing hiking boots or a leather belt, they might still be there, but . . ."

"But her feet . . ."

"It's to be expected, Silas," said Rain. "Feet and hands are usually the first to go. There isn't much of a current in Lake Powell, but there is enough. And it's still fifty feet deep there."

"We've got a dive team going down," said Stan Baton. "But as you know, it's pretty murky down there."

"Was there any evidence that she was, you know . . . assaulted?"

"There is no evidence, Silas." Rain looked directly at him. "But given the state of decomposition, all of our usual tests for this sort of thing won't work. No other bones were broken and this wound suggests that this was a murder, and not an assault that led to murder."

"Does where she was found tell us anything?"

"It could be that the killer dumped her body into the lake in the log debris to keep her hidden below the surface. If that's the case, it worked. It's also possible that during a flood or maybe a storm, her body just happened to become entangled with this material."

"We think there was maybe five or six feet of water over that debris five years ago, Silas," said Baton. "There's been some up and down to the water level, but it's been very low for the last ten years or so, since the big drought. It's possible that there was as little as a foot or two of water covering her."

I never looked there, thought Silas. *I hadn't even* thought *of looking there. It was too far away. If I had, I might have found her.* He shook his head. "But you don't think she was killed there?"

Taylor answered this question. "We haven't recovered any evidence at the scene. We've got a team from Kane County and our own experts combing the area. The Hole in the Rock is a long, narrow passageway that leads from the Jeep track above down into the waters of Lake Powell. It's a big area to search. We've got a special dog team on site and a dozen forensic people. We've been at it for about eight days and so far nothing."

"What are you looking for?" asked Robbie.

"Ballistics."

"Silas, if you want to know anything else, just let me know. I don't have all the answers yet, but we're getting there," said Katie.

"We'd like to ask you just a few questions before we let you go," said Taylor. Silas said nothing and the Special Agent continued. "In the past, we've always assumed that when your wife went for this hike, the one that she was on when she disappeared, she was alone. Now we think maybe she was with someone. Can you think of who she might have been hiking with?"

"Everybody she might have been with is dead," Silas said. "Darcy McFarland, Jane Vaughn, who I found at the Atlas Mill last year, Kiel Pearce."

"What about Josh Charleston?" asked Rain. "Hayduke?"

Silas nodded. "Yes, it's possible. But he and I have been . . . working together, as you know, to try and find Penny. He's helped with these other . . . situations, these other people who have been killed. He got shot last spring while we were investigating Jane Vaughn's murder. I haven't seen him in months; I think he went down to Baja to recover. First he was with his folks up in Seattle, then I got a postcard from Mexico. That's the last I heard from him. If he was with Penny around the time she disappeared, he *would* have said something."

"We'll look into it," said Taylor. "Silas, I know we've been through this before, but we have to ask now that we know that your wife *was* murdered: Can you think of anybody who would have wanted Penelope dead? Did she cross anybody? Did anybody hold a grudge?"

Silas thought about the journal he had found the year before outlining her plans for an Ed Abbey National Monument: the sweeping protected area that would cover so much of the canyon country both she and Abbey loved. He had kept this journal hidden from the FBI. It was a record of all the places she had considered important and worthy of inclusion in a presidential proclamation she hoped would protect the Southwest. In the journal there were notes about developers and others who opposed her, people she considered obstacles to her progress. "I need to think about that."

"Dr. Pearson, we need to take this seriously," said Taylor.

Silas stood up, weary. "Special Agent Taylor, I'm glad that you've just come to this realization, but *I've* been taking this seriously for the last five years. Now, when can I bury my wife?"

5

SILAS AND ROBBIE WALKED OVER to the Moab Diner for lunch and afterward visited the Red Rock Canyon Bookstore, tucked away from tourist traffic and any possible book buyers four blocks off Main Street.

"I've never been here," Robbie said as they opened the door. Silas gathered up a month's worth of junk mail from the ceramic pot by the entrance.

"Really?"

"No; I got here and we went out to Castle Valley and then went down the Green."

Silas turned on the lights that illuminated the two parallel rows of bookshelves. The room was musty and hot. He walked to the back to flick on the air conditioner and took two Dr Peppers from the fridge, handing one to Robbie. Silas sat behind the desk that doubled as a service counter and Robbie took the chair in front of it. The young man looked around.

"You really did just move all your books from Flagstaff and started selling them."

Silas seemed lost in thought. "What? Oh, yes. I thought I needed something like this to keep me busy. I didn't want to be known as the crazy guy who was wandering around the desert looking for his missing wife . . ."

"How'd that work out?"

"Not very well. The nightmares haven't helped. The FBI calls me 'the Dreamer.'"

"What happens when you sell your last book?"

"I don't know. Don't tell Mary at Back of Beyond Books, but I've actually ordered a few new ones to fill in some of the holes on the shelf."

Robbie looked around. "You've got messages," he said, pointing to the blinking light on the telephone.

Silas smiled. Looking at his son, he hit the speakerphone button and then the speed dial option for his messages. There were half a dozen messages waiting for him. After a beep the first one started.

"Hi, um, you don't know me." It was a man's voice. "I mean, we've never met. I live in Colorado. My wife is missing too. I know this sounds crazy but I wonder if maybe you'd, you know, try to dream about her. I know that maybe it doesn't work that way, but I thought I'd try. I just don't know what else to do."

Silas erased the message. "That's the saddest thing I've ever heard," Robbie said, looking down, his voice catching in his throat.

"I get half a dozen calls like that a month. I don't have the heart to call anybody back. I don't know what I'd say."

"SO, DAD, ARE we going to talk about it?" He was looking at the books on one of the shelves.

"Talk about what?"

Robbie sat back down. "What the FBI just told you."

Silas seemed to return from a daydream. "I don't know what there is to talk about. I don't know what to make of this. I always thought I'd find her. I thought she'd be curled up under a juniper and that she would have died of exposure or dehydration, or maybe she would have fallen into a slot canyon and not been able to climb out."

"Even when you started finding other bodies? Didn't this seem, I don't know, inevitable?"

"There was nothing inevitable about it to me. I suppose I figured this was a possibility, but why have all these dreams if someone else is going to find her?"

"I studied criminology, not psychology. I don't have an answer for you."

"I guess I'll need to see my shrink and ask her."

"You're seeing a psychologist?"

"Ken Hollyoak introduced us. He'd been seeing her for years."

"Dad, when the FBI asked if there were people who might have wanted Penelope dead, you didn't say anything, but I knew you were thinking something. What was it?"

"My wife made a lot of enemies, Rob. People around here didn't like her. She had friends, most of whom I never really knew, or even knew *about*, but she made a lot of enemies too. I'd say at the top of that list would be Jacob Isaiah. He's a local business developer. He builds resorts and condos and dabbles in oil and gas. There is Chas Peers, who used to be the superintendent of Glen Canyon National Recreation Area, and his buddy Paul Love, who owns a marina and a powerboat rafting operation."

"Didn't he pull a gun on you last spring?"

"He's the one. He's awaiting trial. He's likely going to get probation."

Robbie shook his head. "Probation for a weapons offense."

"This isn't Canada. His buddy Peers has been transferred from Glen Canyon to a small national historic site in Oklahoma or something. It's the Park Service's way of burying a problem that they don't want to deal with."

"Who else?"

Silas thought a moment. "Well, there is this senator."

"As in, an elected senator?"

"They elect everybody down here. He's a big name in Utah politics. Started in Salt Lake as the mayor, then was governor for two terms, and now is a US senator."

"Does he want to be president?"

"Maybe. I don't know and I don't really care. He's behind almost every conservation disaster in Utah, and a fair number in Arizona, New Mexico, and Colorado. I think he and Penelope clashed a number of times over her proposal for an Edward Abbey National Monument."

"Could he have, you know . . . ?"

"Killed her? I don't see why not. Or had someone else do it."

"Anybody else?"

"I'm sure there is. Her body was found in Glen Canyon but that whole area around where she was found is part of the Grand Staircase-Escalante National Monument. I bet there's all sorts of stuff Penny was involved in that I don't even know about. Maybe that's why she was found there."

They were silent for a while, both men lost in thought. "So, what's with the Edward Abbey connection?"

Silas smiled. "Penny was crazy about him. About his writing. She loved his vision for the Southwest. She was trying to immortalize that vision in a sweeping National Monument that would protect, I don't know, five, six, maybe seven million acres of the Four Corner states."

"How about this Hayduke character? How did he get mixed up in this?"

"Hayduke." Silas said it as a statement. "He and Penny were friends. His name was in the journal I found in the kiva down in Hatch Wash last year. It was scribbled inside of the cover: *Call Hayduke*. I called him and he's been helping me out. He actually saved my life once."

"What do you mean, scribbled? You mean Penelope had left herself a message to call this guy?"

"Yeah. It was written inside the cover and had his cell number.

What was strange was that I had run into him up in the La Sals just the week before, out on an old logging road. I had driven up there to do some thinking, you know, get out of the heat, and there he was. We chatted and I went on my way. I don't think I even got his name that time. It was just for a few minutes. Then the next week I found Penelope's journal. I asked Mary at Back of Beyond and she described this guy to a tee. It clicked. So I called him and we met and it turns out he and Penelope were friends. He's been pretty helpful."

"He knew Penny, as well as Darcy McFarland and Kiel Pearce?"

"Yeah, but I don't know how well. I mean, to hear him say it, he and Penny knew one another pretty well. He calls her *Pen*."

"I can see by the look on your face that you don't like that."

"Would you?"

"I'm just trying to think through the connection between these three open cases."

"Yeah, I've been thinking about that too. The thing that ties these three people together is the Colorado River. Darcy was found near here, at a place called Potash. It's a huge mine site where they are processing potash and shipping it all over the world. It was in Abbey's book *Beyond the Wall*. Kiel was found in Paria Canyon, which flows into the Colorado near Lee's Ferry, in a location mentioned in *One Life at a Time Please*."

"And Penelope was found in Glen Canyon." Robbie saved his father from having to say it.

"Abbey talked about Glen Canyon in many of his books; he hated Lake Powell and the dam."

"You think the three of them were into something that got them killed?" asked Robbie.

"I don't know. But that seems more and more like a distinct possibility."

6

THE CHIME OF THE DOOR saved Silas from thinking too much about the murder of his wife. "We're closed," he called out.

Then he saw it was Katie Rain. "The sign on the door says *Open when I'm here, closed when I'm not.* You're here, aren't you?"

"Not really. Dr. Katie Rain, you've already met Robert Pearson, my eldest spawn."

Robbie stood and extended his hand. "Folks call me Robbie. Thanks for handling things so well back there at the sheriff's office. I appreciate it."

Katie smiled and took his hand. "It's part of the job. I get paid to look at bones, but it's the people who actually count. Your father tells me you're a criminologist."

"I wouldn't say that. I just finished my undergraduate degree at the University of British Columbia, in Vancouver."

"What are you specializing in?"

"I haven't yet. I'm thinking cyber crime is the way to go. It's a huge field, and evolving very quickly."

"Well, let me know if you'd like an introduction to someone at the FBI. We've got the best cyber crime unit in the world."

"Thanks, I might take you up on that."

"How you holding up, Silas?"

Silas motioned for Katie to sit on a stool by the desk. She did. "I'm swinging back and forth between anger and relief. And every time I feel relief I feel guilt, which makes me angry."

"Sounds perfectly normal to me."

"Does it? I don't have any idea what normal is anymore."

"What are you going to do now?"

"Bury my wife. Or more than likely have her cremated and scatter her ashes somewhere. You know, she didn't even have a will. No burial instructions. I'm just guessing that she would have wanted to be scattered over the canyon country somewhere. I know a good place."

SILAS STOOD WITH his hands at his sides, his face a mask of detachment. Before him on his living room wall were the floor-to-ceiling topographic sheets that had become the focus of his world for the last five years. He studied them. Nearly all of the maps before him had been cross-hatched, indicating that he had searched an area once, and then colored in, denoting a second search. He had hiked a distance equal to a walk from San Diego, California, to Bangor, Maine, and back again, and then kept on going out into the Pacific Ocean. He had logged tens of thousands of feet in elevation gain, enough that he could have climbed a set of stairs halfway to the International Space Station orbiting the earth. He was exhausted and feeling every bit his fifty-eight years. Robbie looked into the living room. He took something off the stove, then came in and handed his father a bottle of beer. He had one of his own.

"You should write a book. A hiking guide or something."

Silas smiled wryly. "What would I call it? *A Guide to Finding Dead People in the Desert?*"

"I doubt there are many folks around here who know this place as well as you do."

"They can have it. I'm done." He reached for the map, about to tear it from the wall.

"Wait! Don't do it!"

"Why the hell not?"

"Give it a few days. Give it some time."

"What am I giving it time for? She's dead. Gone. Murdered. What the hell is there left to do?"

"There's a pattern." Robbie pointed to the yellow sticky notes that Silas had left on the Indian Country map that spanned the Four Corner states indicating where Darcy McFarland's, Kiel Pearce's, and now Penelope's bodies had been found.

"Of course. I see it."

"SO WHAT *DOES* it mean?" Silas and Robbie had just finished supper and were sitting at the picnic table watching the last of the day's light evaporate.

"I don't know. The locations are significant, though. They aren't accidental. You told me the FBI have worked up a profile and determined that it's likely that Darcy McFarland and Kiel Pearce were killed by the same person."

"It was because of the intimacy of each crime. The close contact. Darcy had her skull cracked and then was drowned; Kiel had been strangled and stabbed."

"Both of those suggest a level of anger, even hatred, and a close personal relationship. They knew their killer," said Robbie. "He, or she, knew them and hated them. It might not have been the kind of hatred that comes from being jilted or scorned; it could be the result of bad business."

"Kiel Pearce's death was made to look like a suicide. He had been strangled and stabbed in the gut to attract carrion feeders," said Silas. "He'd been hung in a place where the killer knew that vultures would get to him quick, long before he was found."

"That's right. And Penelope was shot at close range. Dad, the angle of the bullet that the FBI describes suggests that she was on her knees."

"I know, Robbie."

"You told me that Kiel had traces of chloroform in his system."

"Darcy's body had been in the potash solution a long time, but Dr. Rain says that the saline solution preserved traces of chloroform. Penny was . . ."

"Chloroform might not have been used on Penelope. Her murder was years before both Darcy and Kiel's. He started with her, and only later added the other two. The addition of chloroform may have allowed him to manage his victims better. We're looking for one guy. One *man*. Someone strong enough to carry a body down the Hole in the Rock. Someone strong enough to smash someone on the head and then submerge them in potash solution. And someone intimate enough with each of these people that they went for a hike with him before they were murdered."

7

"*THE EARTH, LIKE THE SUN, belongs to everyone, and to no one.*
Penelope loved that quote. And she loved this one: *I want to weep,
not for sorrow, not for joy, but for the incomprehensible wonder of our
brief lives beneath the oceanic sky.*" Silas Pearson's hand trembled as
he held a few notes, his weather-cracked fingers clutching the pages
as a breeze tugged at them.

He stood on a jetty of naked stone, a few tangled bushes glowing
orange in the late afternoon sun. Behind him the earth disappeared
into a vacuous space. Fifteen hundred feet below it seemed to
reemerge where the White Rim Plateau, twisted and cut by dry
arroyos, bordered the Green River.

A handful of friends stood on the ledge of sandstone near the
Green River Overlook on the Island in the Sky. Katie Rain was there,
as were Robbie and Stan Baton. Trish Hollyoak wiped tears away,
both for Silas's loss, and her own raw anguish at the loss of her own
husband just a few months earlier. Mary Avery from Back of Beyond
Books held a few volumes of Edward Abbey's prose and Roger
Goodwin, the archaeologist who lived on the Hopi Reservation,
bowed his head in silence. Sarah Jamison, who also taught at UNA,
stood beside Roger. Behind them, his ball cap clutched in his hands,

Dallas Vaughn stood, holding onto his two girls. Jamie Pearson stood nearby, his eyes cast down.

"It's been five years since Penelope disappeared. I wasn't a very good husband to Penny. I was never unfaithful, but I was distracted and distant and never paid much attention to the things that mattered to her. This mattered to her." Silas gestured toward the open space. "This mattered." He stamped his feet. "And this mattered." He held up his notes, referring to Abbey's words scribbled on them. "And as hard as it is for me to accept, *I* mattered to Penny, and it was only after she vanished that I came to see it. I wish I could stand up here and tell you that Penny is at rest now, that her heart is free, and that I'm going to carry on with what she started, carry on her crusade to protect the American Southwest. I can't tell you that. I don't know *what* to do next. What I do know is that Penelope loved the wind, the rock, the sun, the sky, and all that wild country that surrounds us now, and she would have wanted to be remembered as someone who lived life to the fullest—never compromising, never backing down, and never surrendering when something was as important as this is."

Silas let his head fall forward. When he had composed himself, he unfolded the paper clutched in his hand and read, "'*The bird that flies from the night into the lighted banquet hall circles twice around the blazing candles and then flies out.*' That's how Edward Abbey described life. So brief, and so bright. Those lights blazed for Penelope de Silva."

"I'M GOING TO go into Moab before I head back to the Castle Valley," Silas told his sons.

"You want us to come with you?" asked Robbie.

"No, head home. I've just got to get a few things and I'll be there shortly."

Silas drove into Moab and proceeded to the grocery store. In all of his time in the Spanish Valley he had rarely ventured out of the frozen food aisle. Now he picked up a few things to cook his boys a real meal: steaks for the grill, potatoes, and corn on the cob. He paid for his groceries and was loading the bags into the back of his dusty Outback when he heard a voice behind him.

"Looks like you're fixing to have a little party there, Silas."

Silas turned to see Jacob Isaiah behind him. "Hello, Jacob." The old man's face was sun-bronzed, his white hair thin and pasted to his boney head.

"I'm real sorry to hear about your loss."

"That's nice of you to say."

"She was something else, your Penny was."

"I've got my boys out at the place, Jacob. I should be getting along."

"Don't let me stop you. I just was wondering how it came to pass that she was out in the middle of nowhere, that's all."

"I should get going."

"Of course, of course. Funny thing about the Escalante country: a lot of mystics go there to disappear."

Silas finished with his groceries and closed the hatch. He tried to step past Isaiah but the old man blocked his way. Silas looked him in the eye and didn't like what he saw there. Silas narrowed his own eyes, trying to get a read on the broad smile Jacob wore.

"You've got something on your mind, Jacob?"

"No, nothing in particular. But I think you do. I think you got something on your mind and that it's best you just forget about it."

"Listen—"

"No, you listen, Silas. I don't want to speak ill of the dead. That ain't what I'm getting at here, but I know you, I know what you're thinking."

"You have no idea what I'm thinking."

"I do. You're thinking that you ought to find out what your Penelope was up to when she got herself killed. You're thinking that maybe you and your boys might do a little Dick Tracy work. Well, I suggest that you leave well enough alone."

"What business is it of yours?"

"Everything that happens in these parts is my business, Silas. Every goddamned thing. That was something that your Penelope couldn't seem to get through her head." Jacob poked his own creased brow right between the eyes. "She couldn't get that through her thick skull." He poked himself a second time. "Look what it got her. I think it's best that you just leave things alone."

"Do you know something about my wife's murder, Jacob?"

The old man laughed. He sounded scornful. "I only know what I read in the newspapers, but I do know a great deal about your wife's *life*, and she spent it poking her nose into everybody else's business. And like I said, everything that goes on in these parts is *my* business. Now, you go and enjoy your little—what do *you* call it? Celebration of life?—with them boys of yours. But I strongly suggest that you put all of this behind you now." The old man's smile seemed to have been stitched onto his face. His teeth gleamed in the late afternoon sun.

"For the longest time I thought you were involved in my wife's disappearance, Jacob, but after the business with Hatch Wash was settled, I gave up that notion. Listening to you right now makes me start to wonder all over again."

"Maybe I overestimated you, Dr. Pearson. Maybe you're more like that wife of yours than I gave you credit for."

SILAS DIALED HIS cell phone on his way out of town. Katie answered the phone on the fourth ring. "I just got back to Salt Lake City. I'm still in the airport. Is everything alright?"

"Listen Katie, I need to know something. When you were telling Robbie and me about the gunshot wound, you explained that Penny was shot in the frontal lobe. Can you be more specific?"

"Oh Silas, do you really want to be talking about this? What's going on?"

"I need to know. It's important."

There was a long silence. Silas heard a departure announcement in the background over the phone. "She was shot lower down on the frontal lobe, just above the nasal bridge."

"Between the eyes?"

"I guess you could say that. She was shot along the ridge of bone between the eyebrows. So yes, between the eyes. Silas, what's going on?"

"I don't know. I'll let you know when I figure it out."

8

THEY STOOD IN THE EMPTINESS together, a sky shot with lightning and ripped with thunder above them. A bald laccolithic dome sat blue on the horizon; around them the tableland of sandstone was knifed with canyons the color of blood. Wind blew her hair in tatters. She held his hand, and when she spoke, her voice was like a whisper leaking through the storm. "You walked into the radiance of death through passageways of stillness, stone, and light."

"YOU LOOK TIRED, Dad."

"Thanks, Jamie. It's always good to be reminded of that when you're my age."

"You know what I mean. Didn't you sleep? Did Rob and I keep you up?"

"I slept. It just wasn't very restful. Can you stay for the weekend? We could all go hiking together somewhere. Or maybe head across the border to Colorado Springs and find a decent pub that serves real beer. What do you say?"

"I've got to get home, Dad."

"You just got here." Silas realized his voice sounded pleading.

"I know, but I've got to get back to work."

"Stay here. You can work at the bookstore. I'll pay you. You can run it. Be manager."

Jamie stood with his arms folded across his chest watching the sun rise through the floor-to-ceiling windows in Silas's living room. He shook his head. "Thanks for the offer. I've got a job."

"Crewing on a rich man's boat?"

"It's a world-class racing yacht. I'm sailing it to New Zealand."

Silas nodded. "Alright, well, thanks for coming. I appreciate it. You know, I realize that you didn't get on well with Penny—"

Jamie turned around. "It's not that I didn't get on well with *her*, Dad. I got on fine with her. I just resented the fact that I only got to see *you* twice a year. You were my father. I was nine. You left."

"Not *for* her, Jamie. I left because . . . for the university. Penny came later."

"Well, *you* left."

"I never meant to hurt you."

"You may not have meant to, but you did."

"I'll make it up to you."

"How are you going to do that?"

"I could come to New Zealand."

"That sounds great. You and me on a boat for six months." A smile crossed Jamie's face when he said it. "Come to Vancouver when I get back. That would be a start."

"Deal."

"HE'LL GET OVER it. He's already starting. I should know: I did."

"But Jamie isn't you, Rob. He's . . . I don't know. He's got a harder head."

"Are you saying I'm a softie?"

"No, it's not that . . ."

"Don't worry about it. Look, I'll drive him out to the municipal airport. He's got a flight out of Salt Lake tonight. I'll come back and we'll start clearing up some of this stuff if you want. What? What is it?"

"Well, I don't think we should take the maps down quite yet."

"What happened?"

"I'll tell you when you get back. I think I need to go to the Escalante."

EVERETT RUESS WAS twenty years old when he vanished in the Escalante Canyons region of Utah's red rock desert. For several years the young man had made the west's great wilderness his home, traveling on horseback or with a burro, living like a nomad. He ranged from the Navajo Reservation to Yosemite and all points between. He was an artist of exceptional insight and his block prints captured the stark beauty of the American Southwest. In 1934, at the age of twenty, Ruess set out with two pack animals to explore the vast wilderness of the Escalante region. After the Mormons and Major John Wesley Powell, he was one of the first white people to do so. His last camp was near Davis Gulch, not far from the terminus of the Hole in the Rock Road where Penelope's body was found. He was never heard from again.

Ruess's body was never found. In 2009 a grave was discovered near Comb Ridge, close to the place where Silas Pearson himself had nearly met his untimely end the year before, but DNA tests concluded that the body discovered there was not Everett's. The mystery grew deeper.

Silas sat in his bookstore, the lights out, the door latched. The hooded reading lamp on his desk cast a warm light over the book: *Everett Ruess: A Vagabond for Beauty*. Written by W.L. Rusho with an introduction by John Nichols; Edward Abbey wrote the afterword. Silas had several copies of this slender tome in his personal library, now on the shelves of the Red Rock Canyon Bookstore. He was flipping through one now. He read the afterword again:

You knew the crazy lust to probe the heart
Of that which has no heart that we could know.
Toward the source, deep in the core, the maze
The secret center where there are no bounds.

Abbey wasn't much of a poet, Silas thought, but he guessed that the crazy lust to probe the heart of what no heart could know was what propelled Penelope too.

She too had disappeared in the Escalante. That was where the answers would be.

9

"NOW YOU UNDERSTAND WHY WE left your Tempo at home?" Silas asked as he played the wheel of the Outback to maneuver around foot-deep ruts in the road. The landscape stretched out as far as the eye could see in a tableland dotted with buttes and bordered to the south by the Kaiparowits Plateau. The sky was dark, the underbelly of cumulus clouds pressed down so that the summit of the great upland reef was obscured.

"What happens when it rains out here?" Robbie wanted to know.

"This road will get pretty bad."

Robbie grinned. "That ought to be interesting."

"We just passed Davis Gulch," said Silas.

"That little ditch back there?"

"It forms a narrow, and very challenging, slot canyon just downstream, then opens up into a wide grotto that empties into the Escalante River. I've never been down it. We might have to check it out."

"And where are we going now?"

"To the end of the road: the Hole in the Rock."

WHEN THEY CAME to a place where the rough road turned to slickrock ledges and the track showed signs—dark black skid marks from oversized tires—that even off-highway vehicles had a hard time ascending, they parked the Outback and walked. Silas carried his pack, stuffed with his survival gear. Two miles across blowing sand and more ledges and they stood before the opening in the canyon rim. Below them was Lake Powell, its water iridescent blue under the black sky. It had been just over three weeks since Penny's body had been recovered by the FBI; there was no sign that anybody remained at the crime scene. Careful inspection of the area showed, however, where a good number of heavy off-highway vehicles had been parked, and where a helicopter landing pad had been cleared in the brush.

"What is this place?"

"This, my son, is the Hole in the Rock. It was an improvised highway, used only once, by a group of some two hundred and fifty Mormons. In 1880 they were ordered to establish a colony near Bluff, south of Moab, and when they set off from central Utah they didn't know what lay in their path. *This* did." Silas pointed at the rim.

"But these men and woman and children weren't going to let a thousand-foot-deep canyon get in the way of the Lord's work. They blasted their way down, lowering their wagons along the rutted road. There are stories that men were dropped down these cliffs in buckets so they could use hand drills and plant dynamite. Somehow nobody died. Maybe God intervened. They got down the notch, forded the Colorado River, and carried on the other side."

Robbie shook his head.

"There's a place back on the road a ways; you might have noticed it: a big dome-shaped rock. It's called Dance Hall Rock. Those same pioneers held square dances there. They were in pretty good spirits before they saw what lay in store for them."

Silas shouldered his pack and the two men started down the trail through the notch at the top of the canyon rim. The first few hundred yards were easy going, but then they came to steep drops that required the use of their hands to down climb. "They got wagons down here?" asked Robbie.

"Yup, and livestock."

After thirty minutes they were within sight of the water. Silas stopped. There was yellow crime scene tape tangled in a few shrubs. He sat down on the rock and regarded the scene. The waters of Lake Powell—what Abbey called Lake Foul—were just below. On the far side of the stagnant water more sandstone domes rose up on what should have been the inside bank of the Colorado River. It would not have been Penny's first choice for a final resting place. "What *were* you doing here?" Silas asked out loud.

"Did you say something?"

"I was just wondering what Penny was doing here."

"Is there anything in that journal you found?"

"She was always looking for a way to tear down the dam, or drain the lake, and bring back Glen Canyon."

"She might have been meeting with someone who could help her."

"More likely with someone who opposed her."

"You think this is where they found her?"

Silas just nodded.

"You want some time alone?"

By way of answer Silas blindly reached for his son's hand. Robbie let him find it and they sat that way for a long time.

ON THE HIKE back up, Robbie quietly asked, "If she wasn't, you know, killed down there, then where?"

"I've been thinking about that. The FBI have gone over this place with a fine-tooth comb. Metal detectors and whatnot. They didn't recover any ballistics anywhere around the location she was found. Maybe the bullet is in Lake Powell."

"Could be," said Robbie. "But the angle that the bullet, you know, entered her skull, would suggest that if she was killed here, the slug would be in the rocks, not way out in the water."

They reached the top of the rim and made their way back to Silas's car. The storm had blown off, leaving tattered remnants of cloud on the horizon. Between dark anvil-shaped cumulonimbus clouds, rays of light fell to Earth like search beacons. They drove ten miles along the road and stopped at the cut-off to Dance Hall Rock.

"Wanna camp where the Mormons did?"

"Why not?"

They made their way to the informal campsite and set up. After they had eaten, the two men took cans of beer and wandered around the site. The dome of rock made an imperfect dance stage, but it would do, thought Silas.

Robbie prowled around the site. "Hey, Dad," called Robbie.

"Yeah?"

"Did the Mormons set up their camp *on* the rock?"

"I don't know. I doubt it though. Why?"

"Come look at this."

Robbie was on the far side of the massive stone. "What is it?" asked Silas, kneeling.

"That. I thought it might have been an iron spike driven into the stone, you know, where someone had set up a tent. It's too small."

Silas's face was just inches from the stone. There was a one-inch-deep impression in the rock; embedded there was something dark and metallic. He turned to look at his son, the question etched on his face.

Robbie dropped to his knees and put a finger in the rock. The stone was sharp. The metal plug had a smooth finish.

Robbie looked out over the empty desert. "I think we had better call your friends at the FBI."

10

"IT'S NEARLY DARK," PROTESTED ROBBIE.

"I *have* headlights."

"I know. My point is, it's eight o'clock. Who are you going to call?"

"I have Katie's cell. I think I even have Special Agent Taylor's cell. I'll wake them up if I have to."

"It will be midnight before you reach Escalante. We don't know what we're looking at. Even if it is a bullet, maybe some redneck was just horsing around and thought it would be fun to shoot a rock. Some of these folks are a few rounds short of a full clip, I've heard."

"No, this is it. This is the place." Silas was looking up at the curving stone of Dance Hall Rock looming high above him.

"*What* is the place?"

"This is where she died."

SILAS CONCEDED THAT there was nothing that could be done before morning, but he didn't surrender to sleep. While Robbie retreated to their tent, Silas sat on the slab of stone and watched the night sky revolve around him. Sometime in the night he heard a pack of coyotes nearby start to howl and yammer as they moved off toward the Escalante River. Nighthawks and bats took turns divebombing the dark sky for flying insects. He fell asleep on Dance Hall Rock sometime after three and woke a few hours later stiff, aching, and half frozen. As quietly as he could, he lit his stove and made coffee, and as the first hint of morning colored the eastern sky, he stuck his head in the tent.

"I'm heading to town. I'll be back by noon."

"You want me to come?" Robbie asked sleepily.

"Stay here and keep any tourists off the rock."

Robbie nodded and went back to sleep.

BY NOON SILAS had returned to Dance Hall Rock. Within an hour a helicopter arrived carrying FBI agents and their gear: Janet Unger and John Huston from the FBI crime scene identification team along with Dwight Taylor and Eugene Nielsen. Shortly after, members of the Kane County Sheriff's Department arrived. Kane County Sheriff John Danforth, who had been on the Green River when Silas was notified of Penelope's body being found, greeted Silas and asked how he was doing.

The team went to work. They erected a tent over the location of the divot in the stone and photographed it and sketched the suspected crime scene. The tent was then enclosed, and as darkness fell, Unger sprayed the area with a latent blood reagent and exposed the site to ultraviolet light. Tiny hemoglobin particles—able to withstand years of harsh conditions—that had adhered to the slickrock were illuminated by the light.

"You're going to want to see this," Unger called to Taylor, who was standing with Silas outside the tent.

"Give me a minute." Taylor held his hand up.

"I need to see this too," Silas insisted.

"Silas," said Taylor, using his name for the first time that Silas could remember. "You need to let us do our job. Be patient."

Taylor disappeared into the wall tent. Silas could hear him talking with his colleagues. Taylor came out. "It's positive."

Silas started to approach the tent.

"It's a crime scene, Dr. Pearson. We've got to preserve this as evidence, and if I let you in there, it could be used against any case we bring forward in your wife's murder."

"What's in there?"

"It's faint. It's been five years and there's been a lot of weather, but I believe what we're looking at is a lot of blood."

"IT'S BEEN TOO long for us to do some of the things we'd normally do around a crime scene," said Agent Taylor. Silas and Robbie were sitting in folding camp chairs; Taylor stood before them. Sheriff Danforth shifted from one leg to the next beside him. "For example, normally we'd check for tire tracks, for garbage that might have been left behind at the scene, but it's been too long. Hundreds of people have been to this spot since."

"Fingerprints?" asked Robbie.

Taylor shook his head. "There's nothing to take prints from."

"What about the bullet?"

"We're working on recovering it. It's embedded in the rock so we'll have to chip it out. If there's enough left of it we can start running a ballistics match. It's not going to be easy; a slug that deeply embedded in stone will have been flattened. We'll get it to our Firearms and Toolmarks lab at Quantico and see what they can do with it."

"What else are you looking for?" asked Robbie.

"Witnesses," said Taylor. "We know *when* Ms. de Silva disappeared. We can pinpoint her murder to a week-long window. We've been canvassing the nearby towns for anybody who might remember her. She was definitely in Escalante; a few merchants recall her from around that time. We're also going through the Bureau of Land Management's records to see who they sold permits to for that time period, but that's a long shot. This area isn't well regulated, so anybody could have been out here camping and we'd never know it. We're thinking about running a segment on the news, and maybe even on America's Most Wanted, asking that anybody who was in this vicinity and might have heard something to give us a call. It's a long shot, but sometimes we get lucky."

"Can we stay here tonight?"

"You can. We'll be working the scene in the morning," Taylor looked at his watch. "There will be a Kane County sheriff's deputy on site all night. Please don't try to enter the active crime scene; it's really in your interest to preserve its integrity."

Silas just nodded.

"Alright then, I'll see you in the morning."

The light was nearly gone from the sky. Agent Taylor and his team boarded the helicopter and it slowly fired up its engines. Silas and Robbie shielded their eyes as dust swirled around them. Then the helicopter lifted off and flew toward Escalante. The sheriff and all but one of his deputies drove down the Hole in the Rock Road, their taillights blinking in the dark as they navigated the rough track.

The daylight faded and was replaced by a mottled darkness. "You really alright to stay here, Dad?"

Silas bobbed his head. "I know it sounds dumb, but I actually feel a little better being here, you know? I feel closer to Penny than I have in years."

"That doesn't sound dumb."

"Rob, I need you to know: I plan on finding the person who did this," Silas pointed toward Dance Hall Rock and the crime scene tent. "And making them pay."

11

SILAS AND ROBBIE WERE DRINKING instant coffee from tin mugs when the helicopter landed with members of the Kane County Sheriff's Department and the FBI Evidence Response Team. Agent Taylor approached them carrying two large takeaway coffee cups bearing the logo of the Devil's Garden, the local coffee shop and pizza parlor. He handed them to Silas and Robbie.

"I wasn't sure how you took them so you both got cream and sugar."

Silas deadpanned, "After all these years, Agent Taylor, you don't know how I take my coffee?"

"I'm pretty sure you've always declined coffee on all of our previous meetings, Dr. Pearson."

Silas took a sip. It was lukewarm but better than what he had just brewed on his camp stove. He put down his tin mug. "Thank you."

"You're welcome. We've got a specialist with us this morning who will extract the slug from the rock. We're also going to take some of the sandstone to our lab in Salt Lake City to run a comparison on the blood with DNA that we sampled from your wife's hairbrush when she first went missing. That should help us make a positive match between this scene and Ms. de Silva's death. There really isn't going to be much to see, Dr. Pearson. You can both head home."

"We're going to stay in the area for a while."

"I thought you might. I'm going to ask you not to interfere with our investigation, Dr. Pearson. Special Agent Nielsen is heading up the interviews in Escalante. He doesn't need to be tripping over you as he's doing so."

"*Me*, interfere?"

THEY DROVE THE Hole in the Rock Road back toward Escalante. It was well past noon before they rolled into town. Silas gassed up his car and bought beer and then they went in search of food. They found the espresso and pizza joint called the Devil's Garden, named after a local land feature in the Escalante Monument. It doubled as a bookstore and guide-outfitting shop. Silas and Robbie ordered lunch and Silas went to look around the bookstore.

"Help you find something?" asked a big man in a ball cap from behind the counter.

"I wonder if you've ever seen this person around town?"

The man looked at the photo that Silas handed him.

"You're not with the FBI? I just told someone that this lady used to come in from time to time, but it was a while ago."

"I'm not FBI. She is my . . . she *was* my wife. Do you remember when, exactly?"

The man looked at his feet. "I'm real sorry to hear that." He looked up, searching his memory. "Like I told the man from the G, she used to come in here for coffee and a pizza sometimes. This was, I don't know, five, six years ago."

"Do you remember if she was ever with anyone?"

"Yeah, I think she was, but I don't really remember. You know what I *do* remember? She was here once for a town hall meeting we had. Got up and spoke and everything."

"What was that meeting about?"

"About a resort proposal out on the Monument."

"The Grand Staircase-Escalante National Monument?"

"We just call it *the* Monument; saves a lot of breath. She got up in front of fifty townfolks, almost all in favor of this proposal, and tore a strip off the BLM and the folks who wanted to develop it. I think it set things back some, because the folks who were backing the proposal are still trying to get it through the red tape over at the BLM."

"What's the project called?"

"Escalante Resort and Marina."

"What was it all about?"

"You'd have to ask the developer. I seem to remember a big hotel and a marina."

"A marina? The Escalante plateau is a thousand feet above the nearest water."

The man just shrugged.

"Who was proposing this resort?" asked Silas.

"A come-from-away who fancies herself a local now, Eleanor Barry. Come here via a stint in Salt Lake where she spent some time in politics. She inherited a lot of money from her old man who was in oil. She's now into these so-called eco-resorts. A lot of folks around here think it would be good for the town."

"What do you think?"

"I don't care one way or the other. I figure I'm doing alright. But folks want to see more tourists. We've got this massive national monument and not even a paved road to get into it."

"Do you know if this Eleanor Barry is back in town?"

"Back? She never left."

"And the resort?"

"It's still on the books as far as I can tell. I guess the BLM sent them away to do some kind of environmental assessment, but I read last month that they were bringing it forward again."

Silas thought that five years was an awfully long time for a project to be tied up in an environmental assessment. "Do you know how I might find Eleanor Barry?"

"Give her a call. She's listed in the phone book. Runs a real estate business just down the street."

Silas thanked the man and went back to where Robbie was sitting. Their pizza was just being served.

"What did you find out?"

Robbie served his father a piece of pizza. "You're going to find this hard to believe, but Penny *was* well known here. She was butting heads with a local developer. Seems like she caused some considerable delay on a resort project." Silas told him about the proposal.

"Cause for murder?" Robbie asked in a low voice.

"I don't know yet, but I'm going to find out."

"MS. BARRY, THIS is Silas Pearson calling."

"Who?"

"I'm Silas Pearson. We don't know one another, but I think you may have known my wife. Penelope de Silva."

There was a brief pause. "Of course. I saw on the news last night that she was murdered out in the Monument. How terrible. I'm so very sorry."

"Thank you. Ms. Barry, I'm trying to understand why Penelope was out there in the first place. I wonder if you have time to have a cup of coffee with me."

"I don't know how I could be of help."

"Well, I don't know either, to be honest, but I just want to talk with anybody who saw Penelope before she disappeared."

"I suppose I could meet you. Are you in town?"

"I am."

"Why don't you come to my office? I'm on Main Street."

"Can I bring you a coffee?"

"That would be nice."

ELEANOR BARRY WAS a real estate agent who operated an independent brokerage out of a restored farm house on Main Street. She greeted Silas at the door. "Welcome to Escalante, population eight hundred, including dogs and pickup trucks." He offered her hand and Silas shook it.

The inside of her office was warm and decorated with local artifacts and regional artwork. Silas had to admit that the collection of pottery and paintings of skyscapes over the national monument was very tasteful.

Silas handed her a cup of coffee and gave her creamers and sugar in a small bag. They sat down in club chairs in her office.

Barry smiled. She was middle-aged; Silas guessed that she was just little younger than he was; she was fit and attractive and had a gleaming smile. "I knew your wife alright. Not well, but we certainly had our run-ins. The last time I saw Ms. de Silva was at a town hall meeting. This would be five years ago. She walked into a room of local business supporters and, well, ripped us a new one, if you know what I mean."

"I don't. Are you saying that Penelope attacked you?"

"Not personally; that wasn't her style. But we had a little project on the books with the BLM, and Penelope shot it so full of holes it's taken us five years to patch them up."

"Tell me about this project."

"Bill Clinton created the Grand Staircase-Escalante National Monument way back in 1996. He didn't even come here to do it; he went to the Grand Canyon. That's how out of the way this place is. We've been trying to attract some visitors here ever since, but really, except for this little town, and the town of Boulder down the road, there's not much in the way of attractions—"

"Except for the Monument itself."

Barry smiled. "Yes, of course, but our town needs a few tourists each year in order to survive. The environmentalists have chased away all the loggers and miners and oil and gas companies, so we need something to build our economy on, and tourism is it."

"Really?" asked Silas sardonically. He'd heard this so many times over the years he'd been searching for his wife that he was growing tired of the rhetoric. "There's still lots of petroleum exploration in the Monument."

Barry conceded: "There's still *some*. But it's not like it used to be. And every time someone proposes a new well, those hard-nosers over at the Southern Utah Wilderness Association jump up and down on their heads. So, you know, some of us just thought we'd try something different. A green eco-resort. It's going to be a modest vacation spot in the Monument, something that would provide people with a destination for themselves and their families. A hotel, a few condos, a place to moor their boats on Lake Powell."

"That sounds audacious. The only way to get down to Lake Powell from anywhere in the Monument is a two-mile hike after a seventy-mile drive on a bone-rattling road."

"We had an engineering solution to that."

Things came together for Silas. "You wanted to build a road down the Hole in the Rock."

"Not so much a road."

"Then what?"

"A cable car. Like in the Swiss Alps."

Where had he heard this before, Silas thought. "It really is all about water out here, isn't it?"

"We need it to survive, and we need it to make money. There's nothing wrong with that, Mr. Pearson."

"It's Doctor. I'm a university professor. So Penny found out about this and raised some objections."

"Yes, and the BLM took her seriously and sent us back to the drawing board."

"Why five years?"

"We had some homework to do. Our investors had to consider their options. And it's not like this project is the only one we've got on the go right now. We're building in Cedar City, over in St. George, and even in your neck of the woods, in Moab."

"Really, in Moab? I haven't heard your name around town."

"We have other partners. Local businesses people who are the face of our business there."

"Why are *you* in Escalante?"

"Why not? I like this little town. Plus—" She leaned closer to Silas. "My dad did some of the early geological work out here. We lived in town for a few years when I was a kid. I almost qualify as a local." She smiled.

"Do you know where Penelope's body was found?"

"I don't."

He explained.

"That *is* tragic. I am so sorry."

"You don't find it ironic that she was found in the very place that you hoped to turn into a commercial theme park."

Barry shook her head. "That's what Penelope called it. A theme park."

"You don't find it ironic?"

"Dr. Pearson, there is nothing ironic about it. Your wife's death was a tragedy and I am truly sorry for your loss. But *I* didn't have anything to do with it. I think that had circumstances been different, Penelope and I might have been friends. I love to get out in the Monument and explore; I've been doing it all my life. I'm even a fan of Edward Abbey, believe it or not. I know your wife was; she quoted him several times at our hearing. Just because I want to provide opportunities for local businesses to succeed doesn't make me a monster."

ROBBIE WAS WAITING for him in front of the Devil's Garden. "What did you learn?" Robbie started.

"Oh boy, Ms. Barry has quite the set of plans for this region."

"You can say that again! I went over to the BLM office and looked at what they had on file."

"She told me it was a *modest* proposal. Funny definition of modest."

"Dad, they want to build a city in the desert. It's a thousand condos, five hundred hotel rooms, and a paved road to get to it."

"Let me guess: they want to pipe water in from Lake Powell."

"You're getting more cynical as you get older, you know."

"But I'm right, aren't I?"

"Yes, and here's the kicker. The clerk who I got the plans from told me that the reason they've been delaying this for the last five years has nothing to do with the environmentalists, Penelope among them. It's because of the drought. They need Lake Powell full in order to build this floating marina at the base of the Hole in the Rock. It's less than half full now. We have climate change to thank for the delay, he told me."

"You know, I didn't buy the line that the environmentalists had poked it so full of holes that they had to start over. This *is* Utah, after all. I think we need to find out who else had a stake in this project."

"Does the name Jacob Isaiah ring a bell?"

12

ROBBIE AND SILAS WERE STILL standing on Main Street discussing the Escalante Resort proposal when a black GMC Yukon pulled to a stop behind them. Special Agent Eugene Nielsen stepped from the vehicle. He was wearing what Silas had come to think of as his Utah camouflage: a checkered shirt and blue jeans with cowboy boots. He wore his sidearm in full view.

"Agent Taylor mentioned that you were in the region." Nielsen asked what Silas was up to and Silas gave him his perfunctory elusive answer. Nielsen said, "One thing you should keep in mind. Even if this is your wife's murder, Dr. Pearson, you can still be charged with obstruction of justice. I'm certain you have the best of intentions, but if I find out you're withholding evidence, or impeding our investigation in any way, I'll have you charged. That would lead to your deportation. We're clear on that, right?"

Silas didn't answer.

THEY RENTED A room at a hotel on Main Street and moved some of their gear and clothing in.

Silas was standing by the window looking out at the parking lot. "You're pretty good at following the paper trail, aren't you?"

"Yeah—more like the trail of electrons, though."

"You want to get our your electronic shovel?"

OVER BREAKFAST ROBBIE said, "The Escalante Resort is what you might call a mega-project. Five hundred million to start. It involves every conceivable form of summer recreation. The kicker is the water, however. They need to draw water from Lake Powell, so that requires a whole new scale of federal approvals. And they need the reservoir full if they are going to do it, and it hasn't been full in fifteen years. In fact, it's so low right now that a lot of the places people thought were lost forever are above the water now. Maybe you've heard of them: Music Temple, Cathedral in the Desert?"

"Those are supposed to be some of the loveliest places in all the Southwest. Penelope always mourned the fact that she never got to see them. She told me that if they were ever above water again she was going to drag me there, even if she had to tie me up to get me out of the office."

"Well, they're above water now, at least parts of them. And that apparently poses a major problem for the development group. The water level is too low to build this floating marina they have on the books, so they've been advocating for raising the water level. The trouble is, there's something called the Colorado River Compact—"

"The Law of the River."

"This so-called Law of the River says that a certain amount of water has to be discharged downriver, and there doesn't seem to be enough to go around."

"There never has been. The Compact is based on two years of peak flows in the 1920s and the water has literally *never* been that high again. The deal between all of the States the Colorado and its tributaries—especially the Green—flow through divvies up water that is no longer there."

"This group proposing the Escalante Resort want the Compact

changed. They say it's unfair to what they call the Upper Basin States and want it rewritten."

"Where did you find all this?"

"It was filed as a brief to a Senate Natural Resources Committee in DC. One of the senior members of the committee is a Republican senator from right here in Utah—"

"I should have known," Silas interrupted. "C. Thorn Smith. And Jacob Isaiah is backing this?"

"He's *one* of the backers. There are others."

"What's the marina all about?"

"The idea is to have a marina that floats off the shoreline of Lake Powell with moorages accessible via a tram car that descends down the Hole in the Rock."

"That's the craziest idea I've ever heard."

"Maybe, but it's part of the proposal. Paul Love is the lead partner for that part of the project."

"*He's* part of this?"

"His name is still on the development application."

"What a can of worms. We've got Paul Love, who already owns one marina on Lake Powell, and we have Jacob Isaiah, who owns most of the commercial real estate in Moab, both of whom I kept tripping over while I was looking for Penelope. And we have C. Thorn Smith, Utah's favorite son. He was involved in the Darla Wisechild case last year, and his name is on every conceivable development proposal that comes out of the state of Utah. It's no surprise he's backing this."

"It's funny; he is and he isn't. He's in favor of the project, but on the critical issue of water levels in Lake Powell, he's silent. I read through a mile of online testimony on this, as well as everything he's written for the public record, and while he extols the virtue of this resort, when asked about Lake Powell he clams up or changes the subject. That hearing in the Senate: the briefs were prepared and posted, but the committee chair canceled the public testimony into the Compact. I have no idea why."

"Maybe Smith has a soft spot for Glen Canyon."

"I don't think so, Dad. I mean, you might know this senator better than I do, but the only thing he seems to have a soft spot for is relentless boosterism of Utah business."

"So why *is* he mum on one of the biggest business development projects in the state's history?"

"You want me to dig some more on this?"

"Can you? This is great stuff, Robbie. Really great. What else is there?"

"Well, I just dug around online but I can go deeper if I go to the source. There are a few reporters for the *Salt Lake Tribune* that seem to be following this closely. There's also an archive at the paper that I could access if I was there."

"You want to go to Salt Lake?"

"Yeah. Maybe we divide and conquer. I'll head to Salt Lake for a few days; you stick around here and see what you can learn and we'll rendezvous and compare notes."

Silas sat back and looked at his son. "Why are you doing this?"

"I'm hungry. I thought I'd better eat breakfast—"

"That's not what I meant."

"I know what you meant, Dad. Listen, this is fun. I like digging and I'm good at it. And more than that, it's important. It means a lot to you, so it means a lot to me. Look, don't tear up in here. Some of these cowboys might think you're a pansy."

"Why don't we do this: I want to talk with Eleanor Barry again. Now that I know the scope of this thing, I want to get some answers. I also think it's time to pay a visit to some old friends: Paul Love and Jacob Isaiah. We'll swing through Page and then head to Moab. You can get your car and head to Salt Lake for a few days and then we'll decide where to meet. Sound good?"

"Sounds like we're going to ruffle some feathers."

"I'd say that the feathers are already ruffled."

ROBBIE HEADED BACK TO THE hotel to pack while Silas walked down Escalante's main street to Eleanor Barry's office. There was a strong wind that blew Russian thistle, big puffs of tangled tumbleweed, across the road. As Silas walked up the steps to Barry's office he felt like he was headed for a showdown in a spaghetti western.

"Dr. Pearson, how nice to see you again." Barry was standing by the door watching the sky.

"Ms. Barry. I wonder if you would mind me asking you a few more questions."

"I don't mind. Would you like to come in?"

"Why don't we just sit on the porch?" They sat down on rattan chairs. "Ms. Barry, I don't think you were totally honest with me about your project. The scale is massive. You want to build a tram way down the Hole in the Rock."

"It's all a matter of public record. I wasn't trying to hide anything from you when we spoke."

"I suppose that's a matter of debate, but it's not really why I'm here. What's Jacob Isaiah's involvement in this?"

"He's a partner on the project; has been since day one. He has a great deal of experience in this sort of thing and I sought him out both for his deep pockets and for his long history of successful developments around the Southwest."

"Jacob and my wife had crossed swords more than once."

"Dr. Pearson, I don't wish to speak ill of the dead, and certainly not your beautiful wife, but I think if you were to look around you'd be hard pressed to find anybody who proposed any development in the Southwest who didn't cross swords with Ms. de Silva."

"I think her relationship with Mr. Isaiah was particularly adversarial. There was more going on than just developer-environmentalist antagonism."

"How well do you know Mr. Isaiah?" asked Barry.

"He's a frequent customer at my bookstore."

"Come now, Dr. Pearson," Barry laughed, "we both know Mr. Isaiah is no lover of literature. He's a mean, hard-headed man whose only interest is making money and getting his way. Anybody who gets between him and what he wants is bound to suffer the consequences. Jacob doesn't tolerate being obstructed in any way."

"And my wife was an . . . obstruction?"

"She was pretty good at getting in people's way, so yes, I'd say she was."

"And yet, knowing what you do about Mr. Isaiah, you still do business with him."

"I do. And I know how to handle him. He's an old man who lives alone with all his money but with no real friends or family. I provide him with something that he needs more than a bigger bank roll. No, Dr. Pearson, not *that*. I give him vitality, and a sense of direction. I suspect that your Penelope stood in the way of that."

Silas decided to change tack. "What about Paul Love?"

"Ah, Mr. Love. I do believe that it was you, and that hairy friend of yours, who finally pushed him over the edge last spring, wasn't it?"

"He held us at gunpoint. He's involved in your project too."

"Nobody knows the marina business better than Paul Love."

"So here we have two people involved in your project who had plenty of history with my wife, both of whom had more than one reason for wanting her out of the way."

"Dr. Pearson, really? Are you seriously suggesting that either of these men could have committed murder over something as trivial as a resort development?"

"It's not just any resort, Ms. Barry. This is a half-billion-dollar enterprise. For people like Jacob Isaiah and Paul Love, that's more than enough reason to kill someone."

"I've read about you, Dr. Pearson. All those bodies. All those murders. I wonder if you're not starting to look at the world through a very particular lens?"

"Ms. Barry, my wife was *killed*. Her body was dumped below the water line of Lake Powell, where you and your partners want to build a mega-resort, one that has the backing of many of this state's most powerful people, including Senator Smith."

"Smith is no supporter, Dr. Pearson. Sure, he's written some letters and made statements in the press, but what good is all of that without his pull with the Bureau of Reclamation? They control the water in Lake Powell."

"He's been unusually quiet on that matter."

"When we needed him the most, he got cold feet. He's been useless. He's set us back, to be honest. I don't know what argument your Penelope and her band of crusaders made when they met with him, but whatever it was, he clammed up on our proposal, as well as anything that had to do with Glen Canyon Dam and Lake Powell."

"When was this?"

"Shortly after Penelope and her friends appeared at our local hearing."

"Who was there? Do you remember?"

Barry closed her eyes. "There were five. Two woman and three men. I remember that."

"Darcy McFarland?"

"I don't know any of their names. It was Penny who spoke."

"Was one of the men pretty shaggy-looking?"

"No. All three men were pretty clean-cut. One of them was older, and two were young men."

"Can you remember anything else about them?"

"Only that they came together and left together. They seemed pretty tight."

"I don't want to sound like I'm not grateful for this information, Ms. Barry. I am. That being said, I wonder about *your* involvement in all of this."

"I think that's pretty clear . . . oh, wait. You're wondering if I killed your wife, aren't you?"

"Well, you certainly stood to lose a great deal."

"Well, Penelope de Silva certainly caused me a good deal of trouble, and cost the partners on this project a lot of time and money, but in the end the thing that has kept us from building this resort wasn't your wife, or her friends, or all the other environmental groups, but nature. Just when we wanted the water, it wasn't there. And that's the story of Utah, Dr. Pearson."

14

"HOW DID THAT GO?" ROBBIE asked when Silas returned to their hotel room.

"It was surreal. Eleanor Barry is unlike anybody I've ever talked to about Penny. I get the genuine feeling that she feels sorry for me, and that given different circumstances she and Penelope could have been friends."

"Except that she wants to build a mega-resort in a National Monument and insert a drinking straw into a refilled Lake Powell."

Silas filled Robbie in.

"The bit about C. Thorn Smith confirms what I learned reading the correspondence. Why do you think she would be so open about that?"

"Maybe she's angry. Maybe she's feeling frustrated and wants to turn up the heat on him. I get the feeling that Ms. Barry was trying to distract me; you know, look at what the left hand is doing while the right hand—"

"Gets away with murder?"

"I don't know about *that*. Like everybody else involved with this business, she certainly had motive. Just because you stand to lose the opportunity of a lifetime to make a mint doesn't mean that you go out and kill someone."

"I haven't seen anything one hundred percent conclusive on this, but money has got to be the number one motive for premeditated murder, Dad."

"This all seems way more personal than that. The way Penelope was killed, and the others. Drowned, strangled, shot at point-blank range between the eyes . . ."

"It's alright, Dad. Come on, let's get this mess packed up and head out. We've got a known felon to interrogate."

They packed the contents of their room into the back of the Outback. Eugene Nielsen pulled up and stepped out of his vehicle.

Silas walked to the FBI agent. "What can I do for you, Agent Nielsen?"

"Dr. Pearson, Agent Taylor asked me to stop by and talk with you."

"We're just leaving."

"Were you? This will only take a moment. You remember how we discussed interference in our investigation? Well, hard as it is for me to believe, here I am to give you one last warning. You've got to leave this investigation to the FBI. It's come to our attention that you've met with Ms. Barry twice. You are to leave her alone."

"Is she a suspect in Penelope's murder?"

"I'm not here to discuss that. I'm just asking—no, I'm telling you: leave the investigation to us. If you inadvertently compromise an investigation, you might end up allowing someone to get away with a serious crime. Do you want that?"

"No, of course not. But I also am not willing to sit on my hands for another five years while you guys chase your tails."

"Last warning, Dr. Pearson. Next time you'll be getting in the back of my truck and we'll take a long, leisurely drive over to Monticello where you can think about all the time we're wasting incarcerating you while we should be out looking for a serial killer. Understand?"

"I understand your words."

Nielsen slipped his sunglasses back on and shook his head. "It's always so good to talk with you, Dr. Pearson. It's like getting spit in the eye every time."

WHEN THEY WERE driving out of town Robbie broke the silence. "What the hell was that all about?"

Silas gripped the steering wheel so hard that his knuckles turned white. "I have no idea, but I'm going to find out."

"Doesn't it feel as though he's changed his tune? Something must have happened," said Robbie. "Do you think *she* called the police?"

"How else would they know? Unless she called someone *else*."

"Who?"

"Senator Smith. A call from his office to the head of the FBI might set Agents Taylor and Nielsen on us pretty fast."

"Don't you think the FBI would tell the senator not to interfere as well?"

"I don't know. There's a lot of nepotism in Washington right now. I think anything is possible."

"How else would Agent Nielsen know that we were there? She had to have called someone and complained. What is it? Why are you smiling?"

Silas said, "What if the FBI was already watching Eleanor Barry? Maybe that's the reason why they knew I was there. She didn't call them. They were already there."

15

"THIS ISN'T GOING TO BE an easy conversation." Silas piloted the Outback into the town of Page, Arizona.

"How do you want to do this? I could go in and pretend to be a reporter or something."

"He's not going to buy it. He's probably been told not to talk to reporters anyway. No, I think the only way to do this is to be straight up. Maybe he'll spill something. In any case, this could get testy. I wouldn't take your shoes off if he invites us in."

They found the Love residence, and Robbie and Silas walked to the front door and knocked. A woman answered the door.

"Ms. Love, I wonder if your husband is home?"

"Who wants to know?"

Silas looked at Robbie and then back at the woman. "Please tell him Silas Pearson is here."

She closed the door and in a minute came back. "He said for you to leave. I think he's calling the police right now." She started to close the door.

Silas pressed a hand on it. "Ms. Love, I'm sure I'm the last person your husband wants to see right now, but I've just learned that Eleanor Barry is being investigated by the FBI. I think he might want to hear what I know. Can you tell him, please?"

Silas removed his hand and she closed the door. In a moment Paul Love was there. He had dark circles under his eyes and his hair seemed thinner than when Silas had seen him last. "What do you want, Pearson? And who the hell is this?"

"This is my son, Rob." Robbie nodded. "I know you blame me for your situation—"

"Of course I blame you! Look at my hand!" He held up his right hand. It was still blue and disfigured. "Two operations! Six pins! I may never get full use of it back."

"You pulled a gun on me."

"You were accosting us."

"I'm not here to debate with you about what happened at Phantom Ranch, Mr. Love. I thought you'd like to know that another one of your projects is under the microscope. Your development in the Escalante, the one at the Hole in the Rock, is at the center of the investigation into the murder of my wife."

"Jesus, not this again. Is there anybody left in the Four Corners states that you haven't accused of killing your wife, Pearson?"

"I'm not accusing you of killing my wife, but I think that Penelope was in Escalante opposing your resort shortly before she went missing. Maybe you know something about this? The Escalante Resort, I think you were calling it? The one with the floating marina at the bottom of the Hole in the Rock. Your name is on the development application as a partner. Eleanor Barry is being investigated by the FBI."

"Listen, Pearson, I know that you've been under a lot of stress. But all this sleuthing, first about the Vaughn woman and now about your own wife, it's getting out of hand. I think you've gone off the deep end."

"What can you tell me about Penelope and Eleanor Barry?"

"Nothing. There is nothing to tell! They met once or twice at public meetings. I'm sure Barry didn't care for your wife, but that doesn't mean shit. Hell, I don't like *you* but I don't have any intention of killing you. Maybe tossing your ass off my porch, but that's about it."

"This from a man who pulled a gun on me." Love didn't say anything so Silas pressed on. "You had a big stake in this, didn't you? Half-a-billion-dollar project would make one hell of a splash. What was your piece of the project?"

"If you're so smart, look it up. I'm not talking with you anymore."

"Penelope's body was found in the lake, Mr. Love. You're a marina guy; you run a powerboat rafting company. If anybody was going to get rid of my wife's body in Lake Powell, it seems it would be you."

Love just shook his head. "I'm sorry that your wife is dead, Pearson, but I had nothing to do with it. In a few months I'm going to be on trial. I'll see you then." He closed the door.

Silas stood and looked at the door. Paul Love had lost almost all of his bluster in the months since the events at Phantom Ranch. He seemed deflated and defeated.

Robbie waited until he was sitting in the car to say anything. "I think he's telling the truth. I was watching him pretty closely. He made eye contact with you the whole time. He doesn't *like* you, nor did he care much for Penelope, but I don't think he was involved in her death."

"I think you're wrong. Guys like Paul Love know how to lie. It's what they do. He lied about his involvement with the superintendent of Glen Canyon National Recreation Area to block wilderness designation at the Grand Canyon, and I think he's lying now." Silas was driving toward the outskirts of town.

"I'm just saying that he wasn't doing the things we usually look for to see if someone is lying—the eyes looking up and to the left. It's what's called a visually contracted image. When you lie about something you often try to imagine the lie, and create a picture in your head. If you look up and to the right, you're accessing a memory of something. Left means lie. Right means remember. Also, there was his body language. Did you see how he was fidgeting with the door while we talked, and shuffling his feet? A person who is lying usually becomes stiff and rigid; it's part of their effort to control the situation. Love was flopping like a fish out of water. He didn't want to talk with us, but I don't think he was lying about his involvement with Penelope."

"This is what five years of education has got me? A kid who is an expert on lying?"

"This is handy stuff," he said.

"If he wasn't lying, what do we make of what he said?"

"One thing was helpful. He told us to 'look it up.' I think there is a lot more information on what Love, Barry, and this friend of yours Isaiah were up to in the desert than we know about, a bunch of stuff on paper that we haven't accessed."

"So we stick to the plan. We'll head to Moab in the morning and you can get your car from my place."

"Where are we going now?"

"I know a place out in the desert. I camped there a few times last year. It's nice. You can't smell the power plant from there."

After replenishing their supplies they drove through the fading light to the location where Silas had camped the previous spring and set up their tent. Robbie started dinner while Silas gathered wood for a fire. As the sun set it cast long shadows across the desert and illuminated buttes and cliffs far in the distance.

After eating and chatting, they watched the fire burn down. Before turning in Robbie said to Silas, "Does anybody else ever come out here?"

"I'm sure they do, why?"

"I thought I saw headlights, that's all."

"Where?"

"Off in that direction. It was only for a minute."

"It could have been some lights from Page."

"I don't think so."

"Do you see anything now? Maybe it was just someone driving back from his hogan. This is part of the Navajo res."

"Maybe that's what it was. Let's get some sleep, Dad."

Silas sat up for a long time after his son had gone to sleep, looking across the horizon of the desert. He felt a sense of paranoia he hadn't experienced for many months. It was like something or someone was waiting for him beyond the tangle of darkness, but remained just out of view.

16

THEY LEFT EARLY AND HEADED back to Utah. While driving through Blanding, Silas jerked the wheel and pulled the Outback to the curb.

"What is it?"

"Did you see that banner?"

"I missed it. What was it?"

"Senator Smith is in town today. He's at some kind of dedication ceremony. I feel a sudden surge of civic pride."

"You don't even live here! Did you know about Smith being in town?"

"It's pure coincidence. Really."

Robbie didn't believe him and told him so.

The event was taking place at a tree-shaded park on the western edge of town. "You're going to land in jail if you're not careful," said Robbie.

"I'll keep my nose clean. Smith and I have never met face to face so we should be fine."

"'I'll be *fine*.' You'll be in the clink. You think his staffers don't know who you are?"

"Listen, we're here, and he's here. Eleanor Barry said there was something that kept him from supporting her plans. Maybe it was something that happened between him and Penelope's gang of friends. Don't you want to know what that is?"

Robbie went along with his father. The event was billed as an open forum on water in the west. A decade of drought had left Utah parched, and while Smith was adamant in his denial of climate change, he didn't let that get in the way of pontificating about the needs of his constituents for more water.

While there were microphones set up in the grassy park, it didn't seem like the small crowd in Blanding had much to say on the matter—not that the senator let them get a word in edgewise. For almost an hour he held forth about the need to harness the latent potential for growth and prosperity that Utah's water provided. *What water?* Silas kept thinking.

There were a few questions, but the crowd—worn out from being in the hot sun—drifted toward a table of lemonade and cookies as the senator shook a few hands. Silas angled toward him.

"Good speech, Senator."

"Thanks for coming today," Smith said as he shook his hand. If the events of the last year had taken a toll on the man, it didn't show. He *looked* presidential, his hair neatly combed and dusted with gray, his crisp white shirt rolled up at the sleeves.

"I wonder if you have a few minutes to talk."

"If this is an issue about a federal program, you might want to take it up with your congressman. I can get you his number."

"It's not about a federal program. Sir, have you heard of a project called the Escalante Resort?"

Smith hesitated only a second. "Yes, it's east of the Town of Escalante, isn't that right?"

"That's correct, sir. It's been on the books for about five years now. It's a big project."

"I believe I've written a letter in support of it."

"I think that's correct. Do you know the proponents of the project?"

"Remind me, are you with the press?"

"No, sir, I'm just a concerned citizen."

"We're going to have to make this quick, Mr. . . . ."

"It's Dr. Pearson. I believe you knew my wife, Penelope de Silva." Silas waited to see if there was a glimmer of recognition. If there was, the senator disguised it well. "Sir, do you know Eleanor Barry?"

"Name sounds familiar." Now Smith looked around for an aide.

"She is currently under investigation by the FBI. She's the lead proponent of the project."

"What's she being investigated for?"

"I don't know. What I do know is that she claims to have your support for this project."

"Well, I write a dozen letters a day in support of businesses across the state. Haven't you and I met before?"

"I don't think so, sir."

"No, I know you from someplace." The senator seemed to be accessing a file of names and faces in his head. "*You* broke into my office last year."

"There were never any charges laid. You'll recall that your assistant caused me some . . . inconvenience."

"There's a restraining order in place. I could have you arrested just for standing here."

"Be my guest."

"I don't have time for whatever game you're playing now, Pearson. You'll have to excuse me."

"Sir, my wife was found murdered near where the Escalante Resort was to be built. She had been at a public hearing just a few months before. She and her friends were trying to stop the project. I think that the people you are supporting may have had something to do with it."

"Tell the FBI. My involvement in that scheme was just a letter, one of a thousand my office writes every year."

Robbie stepped forward. "Senator, that's not entirely true. You've gone way beyond writing a letter to the regulator. You've pressured a number of federal departments to get behind the development. You've written many letters to the BLM accusing them of being anti-business—"

"The BLM have turned into a bunch of tree huggers. And all I've done—"

"Why have you pressured every other federal agency about this project except for the Bureau of Reclamation?" Silas asked.

"What are you talking about?"

"This project needs water. They need it for the resort and they need it for the marina that Paul Love wants to build, and yet you have been silent on that matter. You used to be a booster for Lake Powell, and five years ago you clammed up on the matter."

"I haven't! Gentlemen, you mistake a few letters for something that actually has my undivided attention. My aides write letters on my behalf a dozen times a day. If we failed to pen one to the Bureau of Reclamation insisting that they refill Glen Canyon Reservoir, then that's an oversight we shall have to remedy. Now, I have to get to Monticello to make another presentation on the vital matter of water in this great state. Excuse me."

The senator walked off toward a waiting SUV. Two aides accompanied him. Even from a distance Silas could hear the aides being dressed down for not coming to the senator's rescue.

"You don't need any fancy training to tell *he* was lying." Silas watched the senator's vehicle speed off.

"How can you tell?"

"I didn't have to tell him that the letter to Reclamation *should* have advocated for refilling Lake Powell. For him it was pretty much top of mind. I wonder what's really behind Senator Smith's current interest in water."

17

THE HEAT IN MOAB WAS fierce. A few cool days earlier in the month of October had given way to a resurgence of autumn heat; when Silas and Robbie drove into the Spanish Valley at the end of the day the temperature was still ninety degrees. Thunderheads rested on top of the Poison Spider Mesa like dark clots of soiled cotton. In the distance, virga trailed behind a bank of cumulus clouds over Arches National Park, the water vapor never reaching the ground.

"We're not going to your place?"

"Got to pick up some groceries and some beer first. I also thought I'd check and see if Jacob Isaiah was in his office."

"You don't think you've had enough for one day?"

"I'm not some decrepit old man—"

"That's not what I mean, Dad. Don't you think you've stirred the pot enough?"

"Not until I get some answers."

After shopping, Silas drove north into the downtown.

"You mind if I check on the store?"

"Only if there's a cold Dr Pepper in the fridge."

They stopped at the store, Silas checking his email.

"Why don't you have a computer at your house?" Robbie sipped his soda and browsed the titles on the shelves.

"Same reason I don't have a phone. Don't need one."

"How many books you got in here, Dad?"

"About seven thousand."

"It's nice. The store, I mean. The wood beams, the old adobe, the lighting. It's tasteful."

"I tried to imagine what Penelope would have done."

"She would like it, Dad."

Silas threw Robbie the keys and left to walk the four blocks to Jacob Isaiah's office. "Pick me up in an hour?"

"I might go and have a beer at Eddie's."

Silas walked through the late afternoon sunshine, the heat rising in waves off the asphalt. He caught Jacob Isaiah just closing up his office. "Good evening, Jacob."

"Not tonight, Pearson, I'm in no mood for the likes of you."

"And to think that just last week you were wishing me well and giving me condolences for my wife's death."

"Well, that was then."

"And this is now. I've spent the last week out in Escalante."

"You don't say. What a surprise. Just like I said, you can't leave well enough alone."

"How is your investment in the Escalante Resort doing, Jacob?"

"That's a private business matter, Pearson; it's no interest of yours."

"But it seems that it is. Did you know that Eleanor Barry is being investigated by the FBI?" It was pure supposition, but so far he had been able to make it work to his advantage.

"That's ridiculous, Pearson. Once more, you have no goddamned idea what you're talking about."

"Don't I? How is it that the FBI knew I'd been out to talk with her? Maybe she phoned them, but if she felt as if I were harassing her, she'd call the sheriff's office, don't you think? Get a faster response.

But sure enough, not two hours after Ms. Barry and I had a lovely chat—our second, I might point out—on her front porch, along comes the FBI to warn me away from her. Why do you think that is?" Silas was walking alongside Isaiah down Main Street.

"You had better leave this alone, Pearson."

"Or what? You'll pop me in the head? Like this?" Silas poked his own forehead between the eyes. "You own a gun, Jacob?"

"I own plenty of guns. If you don't stop badgering me, Pearson, I'll have good reason to use them. The district judge for this region is a golfing friend; he'll be happy to see it as self-defense."

"Is that how you justified killing Penelope? Self-defense? Was she *attacking* you? Was she disrupting your plans to build another resort in the middle of nowhere? Did she come between you and the American dream?"

"You're fucking crazy, Pearson, you know that?" Isaiah crossed the street to the plaza where Eddie McStiff's beer parlor was.

"How much are you in for?"

"None of your business. Now," Jacob stopped at the door of McStiff's. "This is a members-only club, and you are not a member."

"I am, actually. I own a business in town; I'm a member in good standing. Tell me, Jacob, did you do it yourself or have someone else do it?"

"Get the fuck away from me, Pearson!" Jacob pushed past Silas, out of the blazing heat and into the cool of the bar.

Silas followed him. "Penelope was threatening your project. She had you over a barrel on water supply, didn't she? There was nothing you could do. You couldn't make your case to Senator Smith; he wasn't listening. For the first time ever, *he* wasn't listening to *you.* Why was that, Jacob?" Silas was right behind him, so close that he could smell the man's perspiration.

Jacob wheeled on him. Despite being in his seventies he was still quick and strong. His fist caught Silas in the chin and Silas careened backwards. Several patrons in the bar jumped up and a woman shouted. Silas caught himself before he fell. He felt hot and his vision seemed to narrow. In front of him was an old man, his hair now wild and in disarray, his face a mass of disjointed lines. Silas started to lunge toward him when someone caught him around the middle and yelled "Dad!"

Silas stopped. Robbie was grappling with him. Jacob Isaiah pushed his hair back into place and whipped the spittle from his mouth with the back of his hand. "If I ever see you again, Pearson . . ." He let his words trail off into the quiet bar.

"What, Jacob, you'll kill me? Like you did Penelope?"

"Dad, let's go."

Silas relaxed and Robbie let go of his father. The patrons in the bar slowly drifted back into conversation.

Jacob Isaiah spat on the floor at Silas's feet, wiped his mouth again, and walked into the darkness.

Silas and Robbie walked back out into the heat. "Holy shit, are you okay?"

Silas wiped his own mouth; his hand came away bloody. "I'm alright."

"What were you going to do?"

"I don't know. I just saw red. It was like in some cheap paperback when the protagonist loses control."

"Have you ever been in a fight?"

"Do sternly worded arguments over the meaning of allegory in contemporary Western literature count?"

"No, they do not."

18

THERE WAS A BUM ON the steps of the Red Rock Canyon Bookstore when Silas and Robbie arrived the next morning.

"That's not—?"

"It *is*," said Silas when they stepped out of the Outback.

"Holy Christ, would you look at you!" roared Hayduke as he stood up.

Silas extended his hand. "Good morning, Josh."

"Hey, yeah, good morning to you too!" Hayduke embraced Silas and lifted him off his feet. He put the man down and turned to look at Robbie.

"Josh, this is my son, Robbie."

"Well, I'll be damned. Sweet Jesus, I've heard a lot about you!" Hayduke extended his hand and Robbie shook it. Hayduke held his hand tightly.

"And I've heard a lot about you," said Robbie, pulling his hand away.

"Name's Hayduke. As in George Washington Hayduke."

"So I should just call you George?"

"No, fuck no, just Hayduke will do."

"You look different," Silas said, unlocking the door. "You got a haircut and trimmed your beard."

"Yeah, had to. Hospital." He tapped his leg.

"And how *is* your leg?"

"It's good! Real good. I can run, even. Not for long, or very hard, but then I wasn't ever much for sprinting. I'm slow and steady."

Silas stepped into the bookstore, followed by Robbie and Hayduke. "You got any beer?"

"It's ten in the morning." Silas sat down at his desk.

"Shit, already? We got to get started."

"How long were you waiting out there?"

"I don't know, all night I guess. I slept under the cottonwood."

"I have neighbors, Hayduke."

"Nice ones too. Gave me coffee this morning."

Silas shook his head. "Not that I'm not happy to see you, but what are you doing here?"

"Well, my leg's all better, and it's time to get back in the game, I guess."

"Josh, you heard about—"

"About Pen? Fuck yeah, of course. Shit, I'm really sorry. They had newspapers and the web and everything where I was."

"Where was that?" asked Robbie.

"I was in a hospital, man, didn't your old man tell you about that?"

Robbie just nodded.

"I got here as quick as I could. Thought you could use some help tracking down the motherfucker who did this to her. I didn't know you already had a sidekick."

"Son, not a sidekick," said Robbie.

"Whatever. I been along on this ride from the start, man. Silas here found me up in the Mante LaSals and we've been a team ever since. Where you been?"

"At school, in Vancouver."

"What you study? Fine arts?"

"Criminology."

"A real live sleuth. You find the killer yet?"

"We're working on it."

"What you got so far?" Hayduke turned to look at Silas for his answer.

Robbie filled Hayduke in.

"That fucker, Love, is still on the lam?"

"He's out waiting for his trial. Didn't you get a notice to appear? You must have been called as a witness."

"Who knows? I don't have a mailing address. I haven't seen any US Marshalls waiting to escort me to the trial."

Robbie continued, and for five minutes Hayduke nodded, paced, and ranted about developers ruining the Southwest and how Lake Powell was the foulest, most hideous monstrosity ever created by man. "I mean, have you seen Glen Canyon? Have you?"

"Only pictures," admitted Silas.

"Have you?" asked Robbie.

"No. The fuckers stole it. From me, from you, from your father, from all of us. Me and Pen were going to get it back."

"But isn't it back now? Most of it, I mean?" asked Robbie.

"No!" Hayduke roared and slammed his fist down on a bookshelf. Several books hit the floor. "No," he said more calmly as he bent awkwardly to pick them up. "There is *no* compromise on Glen Canyon. That's how we lost; that's how they got it in the first place. There's no compromise on getting it back."

Hayduke put the books back on the shelf, backwards and upside down. When he had paced back and forth a few times inside the store like a wild creature, he said, "We going to catch this fucker. You really think it's Isaiah?"

"He's pretty pissed." Silas rubbed his mouth.

"That old fart actually hit you?" asked Hayduke. Silas nodded sheepishly.

"We need to figure out why," said Robbie.

"Greed, man, plain and simple."

"Maybe, but I would like to find the paper trail. Maybe it was Isaiah who, you know . . ." said Robbie.

"Pulled the trigger?" blurted Hayduke.

Robbie winced.

"Fuck, sorry, I'm such an oaf."

"Glad *you* said it. But yes, maybe Isaiah did it, but who else was involved?" asked Robbie.

"That chick in Escalante?" Hayduke was still pacing.

"Maybe Eleanor Barry was involved. But I want to know what Senator Smith is hiding," said Silas.

"Well, shit, let's go and put the hurt on him!"

"We cornered him yesterday. He's surprisingly cagey on the matter of Lake Powell."

"Maybe he has an ounce of common sense," said Hayduke, grinning.

"What do you mean?" asked Silas.

"Nothing—just that this guy can't be for absolutely everything that is evil in the world, can he?"

"I wouldn't put it past him." Silas turned off his computer and stood up.

"So, what now?" repeated Hayduke.

"I'm going to Salt Lake in the morning," said Robbie.

"And I'm going to spend another day or two around here watching Isaiah, and then head back to Escalante. We can meet up there."

"Yeah, that sounds good! Let's celebrate tonight! The three amigos! I'll get some steaks. You got a BBQ out at your place?"

"Sure. A grill, at least."

"Perfect."

"Yeah, *perfect*," said Robbie.

19

HAYDUKE WENT TO GET STEAKS for the BBQ, and after sharing his concerns over Hayduke's mental state, Robbie said he was going to dig around the county office to see if he could learn more about connections between Jacob Isaiah and Senator Smith. That left Silas alone for the first time that day to contemplate matters. He spent the afternoon in the bookstore absorbed in thought.

Jacob Isaiah was an angry man. His anger seemed beyond what might be fueled by frustration with an environmentalist bent on protecting landscapes he wanted to develop; it seemed personal. Silas looked at his watch. It was almost six. By now Isaiah would have left his Main Street office and retired to his ranch on the plateau south of town. Silas rubbed his chin and felt the raw bruise there. He had pushed things; he had been pushing things since learning that Penelope had been murdered—no, executed. He would keep pushing things until he found out who killed her.

THE SUN WAS setting when Silas stood by the back door to the two-storey Main Street building that housed Isaiah's office. He felt a wave of déjà-vu; it had been a year ago that he had broken into Senator Smith's office. He had learned an awful truth that night, and it had nearly gotten him killed. Silas felt a wave of nausea flood over him and wondered if maybe he should just drive out to his place in the Castle Valley and forget about this. Instead he pulled a crowbar from his bag and looked around the quiet alley, then jammed it into the frame of the door. Using a mallet, he pounded the crowbar into the loose door jamb and pried the door open. The lock popped and pieces of metal and wood fell to the ground. With another cautious look around Silas slipped into the building. He fished his headlamp from his bag and headed up the stairs that led to the second floor.

The building was old and the floor creaked. Silas hoped that the shopkeeper in the art gallery below wouldn't wonder who was using the back entrance at this time of night. He reached the top and quickly found the entrance to Isaiah's land development office behind a locked, large, glass-paneled metal door with Isaiah's name stenciled on them. Silas used the same technique to open this door. He didn't expect an alarm and didn't hear one. He returned his tools to his backpack and stepped inside.

The first thing he realized was that he could hear everything from the shop below. There was soft music playing, a piece from Kristen Larsen's *Canyonlands Suite*. He could hear the owner of the art gallery—a man named Lars Gorman—talking with a patron. It sounded like they were in the room with him. He walked on the balls of his booted feet into the room.

The room was sparsely furnished. There were only two desks and a large, cluttered conference table at the center of the space. Two windows adorned with plastic venetian blinds looked out onto Main Street. Even though Jacob Isaiah was one of the wealthiest men in Grand County, and in the top one hundred in Utah, his frugality—downright stinginess—was legendary. The office appeared not to have been refurnished since the 1970s.

The two desks were on opposite sides of the room. Silas first went to the one on the southern wall and quickly determined that it belonged to Isaiah's assistant. There were two framed photographs of smiling children on the desk, and Silas knew Isaiah was childless. He quickly rifled through the desk anyway, looking for a file or paperwork that might contain something on Penelope. The computer on the desk was at least five years old and Silas dared not turn it on; if it was anything like his own ancient desktop machine it would wake the dead.

He quietly crossed to the other side of the room to Jacob's desk. He heard the shop owner below laugh loudly. The man continued to speak and Silas started breathing again. He reached the desk; it was sparse. No photos; no computer. Just a desk blotter, a phone, a few notepads and pens. The only personal item on the desk was an award from the Moab Chamber of Commerce for businessperson of the year. Silas suppressed a laugh. He opened the drawers in Isaiah's desk one at a time. He did it slowly so they wouldn't make any noise.

In the first two drawers he found nothing but more pens, most of them taken from hotel rooms in small towns around the state. He found a few from the same hotel he and Robbie had stayed at in Escalante.

In the third drawer he found a set of files, neatly hung in a file rack, each bearing a label typed on an old-fashioned typewriter. He fanned through them; each file was half an inch thick and bore the name of a project Isaiah was involved with. He found the project file from Hatch Wash, south of town, where Silas had discovered plans for another of Isaiah's elaborate resorts. Then he found the Escalante project file. He pulled it from the drawer and opened it on the desk. Neatly typed pages of notes, a copy of the summary of the project description submitted to the BLM, pages of correspondence. All of this confirmed what Silas already knew: this was Jacob Isaiah's coup de grâce, his crowning achievement, and it would be the death stroke for a wild and beautiful landscape. Except for a few heretofore unmentioned details—Silas found particular irony in the proposal to create a summer festival at Dance Hall Rock—there was little new in the file. A short letter from Senator Smith explained that for the time being all discussions on water withdrawals from the Colorado River were on hold while the Bureau of Reclamation discussed the future of storage in Lake Powell.

There wasn't a single mention of Penelope.

Silas returned the file to its place and closed the drawer. There was a final drawer, but Silas had lost hope he would discover anything that would help him link Isaiah to Penelope's death. He slid the drawer open. The desk was old and in bad shape, and as he pulled the drawer out it slid off its runner and landed with a heavy thud on the floor. Silas stopped; he felt his heart race. He thought, over the sound of piano music below, he heard Lars Gorman pause in his pontificating about local artists.

He looked down at the contents of the drawer. More files. There were maybe forty files in the drawer, each also with a neatly typed label, but instead of names of projects there were names of people. He found a file for Dexter Willis and another for the mayor of Moab and one for the chair of the local development corporation. There was one for the owner of the *Canyon Country Zephyr*, the local newspaper, and one for Tim Martin, whom Silas had run across in the Hatch Wash business the year before.

There was a file for Jane Vaughn, whose murder Silas had helped solve the previous spring, and for Darcy McFarland, whose murder at nearby Potash remained a mystery.

Senator C. Thorn Smith had a file. Silas quickly scanned it. There were records of donations going back more than two decades, from the time that Smith had run for governor. Smith had been in Jacob Isaiah's pocket for a long, long time.

Silas looked but couldn't find a file on Kiel Pearce, whose murder was also open and unsolved. Nor was there a file on Josh Charleston. There were other names in the files, most of which Silas recognized as belonging to local politicians or bureaucrats with the Forest Service, the BLM, or the Parks Service.

Penelope's file was thicker than all the others. Silas pulled it from the drawer. In the glow of his headlamp he opened the dossier.

Like all the others it contained copies of correspondence. Silas recognized some that Penelope had sent to Jacob, and some that he had sent back. While hers were long and detailed, outlining her concerns with his development projects around the Southwest, Isaiah's responses were curt, bordering on rude. Silas scanned them. There didn't appear to be any overt threats, merely a resignation that people like Penelope had to be dealt with in order to do business in Utah.

After Silas had finished reviewing the correspondence, he found photocopies of newspaper articles where Penelope was quoted criticizing Isaiah's projects. There were a few from the local paper and several from the *Salt Lake Tribune*. There was nothing new in these stories, though Silas found it interesting that Isaiah had underlined or circled several comments that Penelope had made about the Escalante project.

What Silas found next sent a chill up his spine. There was an envelope of photographs at the back of the file. Silas laid them out on the floor next to the drawer. A dozen in total, they were eight-by-ten black-and-white images printed on glossy photo paper. There were several closeup photos of Penelope speaking at a microphone at a hearing or public presentation, maybe even the one in Escalante just a few months before her disappearance. And there were candid photos of her taken with a long lens: Penelope walking toward Ken and Trish Hollyoak's home in Moab; Penelope standing on the street in front of Back of Beyond Books; Penelope through the window of a Main Street Moab diner. There were several of Penelope with Darcy McFarland taken outside what looked like the BLM visitor center in Escalante.

Silas's hands shook as he studied the images. He felt bile rise in his throat. There, in an envelope in this angry man's drawer, were photos taken of his beautiful wife, several of them just months before she was executed in the desert. He fumbled and put the images back in the envelope, tearing the corner of the manila paper. His hands were sweating and he realized he had forgotten to wear gloves. Using the corner of his shirt, he rubbed the envelope, leaving a greasy smear there. He put the files back into the drawer, quickly scanning to see if he recognized any other names. None of them looked familiar, so he lifted the drawer and slid it back into place.

Silas reached the door and as he opened it he used the tail of his shirt to smear any fingerprints he might have left behind. He closed it, making no effort to conceal the damage he had done. What could he do? He started down the stairs, turning his headlamp off as he descended. The first few stairs were silent but halfway down he stepped on an old board that groaned under his weight. He hurried down, wiping fingerprints from the ruined outside door as he exited the building.

The alley was empty and the street was quiet. He drew a deep breath as he walked from the recessed door and made for the sidewalk. He thought he was home free when he heard a voice call after him. "Silas? That you?"

20

SILAS CONTEMPLATED BREAKING INTO A run, but stopped, fixed a smile on his face, and turned to see who was calling him. It was Lars Gorman.

"Silas, what are you doing here?" Lars said, looking around. He was a narrowly built man dressed in tan slacks and a printed shirt. His dark-rimmed glasses were placed atop a full head of black curly hair.

"Oh, hi Lars. I was just, um, finishing up some business downtown."

Lars looked behind him again and nodded. "Business. Alright, I see."

"Yes, my son is in town and I'm heading back to my place now."

"Silas, was that you upstairs?"

Silas felt a lump in his throat. He stared at the man, willing himself to continue eye contact, to not look up and to the left. "No, I was just making my way back from the bookstore—"

"From which bookstore, Silas?"

"From Back of Beyond."

"Silas, you're not a very good liar."

"Look, Lars—"

"Let me see what's in your bag."

"Lars—"

"Your bag, Silas." Lars took a step toward him. Silas towered over him, but something in Gorman's voice was disarming. Silas slipped his bag from his shoulder. Lars opened it and took out the prybar. Lars looked at him with a silly grin. "Really, Silas? A crowbar? Did you find what you were looking for?"

"Lars, I don't know what you mean."

"Silas, everybody in town knows what's going on. Well, mostly everybody. But you've got to take it easy. You can't break into Isaiah's office and not expect him to connect the dots or call Dexter to arrest you."

Silas looked down at his feet. When he looked up, Lars was walking toward the back of his gallery where there was a door adjacent to the one that gave access to the second storey. There was a heavy window in it. Lars swung the crowbar at it and smashed it to pieces.

"Jesus, Lars, what are you doing?"

Lars laughed and handed Silas back the prybar. "Now when Dexter sends someone to investigate it will look like whoever broke in upstairs was just looking to hit local businesses. Now go find out what happened to your wife, Silas."

21

"I'M GOING TO SLEEP UP in the mountains tonight," announced Hayduke after the BBQ.

"You're alright to drive?"

"Shit yeah; even with this Canadian beer, it's no problem. So, tomorrow, you need any help with Isaiah?"

"I'll be fine. I've got to spend some time at the store, maybe sell a book or two, and do some digging."

"Alright, then I'll see you in a couple of days. We'll head to the Escalante."

Hayduke raced off into the darkness toward the La Sal Mountains. Robbie looked at his father standing in the doorway. "I see what you mean."

"Yeah, it's like he rehearses the lines or something, right out of *The Monkey Wrench Gang*."

"You think he's . . . stable?"

"Are you kidding me? He's a loon. But he *has* been helpful. He saved my life on Comb Ridge. He took a bullet on the Arizona Strip."

"I just hope he doesn't get you killed. He seems reckless."

"According to Agent Taylor, he's got a record—assault, I believe.

I think it happened after he got back from the Persian Gulf, some sort of PTSD thing."

"Be careful, Dad."

"Listen, I didn't say anything while Josh was here. I just didn't want him going off on another tangent. The reason I was late coming back from town is I paid a visit to Jacob Isaiah's office. He wasn't there. I sort of broke in."

"Dad!"

Silas told his son what he found. After they had discussed it, Silas sat back on one of the chairs in the living room, looking out into the darkness. "I think we're beyond careful now."

ROBBIE LEFT FOR Salt Lake City the next day. He promised to call Silas on his cell when he got to the state capital. Silas spent part of the afternoon reorganizing and cleaning his gear and getting set for a return trip to the Escalante. Late in the afternoon he drove into Moab, the afternoon light reflecting off the cliffs of Hal Canyon onto the back of the sleepy Colorado River. Silas mused as he drove: it was all about this river, all along. All that time spent scrambling around the plateaus and mesas and canyons, and in the end the answer was just a few miles from his home in the Castle Valley and his store in Moab. The Colorado was what tied Penelope's death to that of Darcy McFarland and Kiel Pearce. In his quest to understand what happened to his wife, he couldn't lose the thread that tied all three of these people together. He wouldn't forget them.

Silas arrived in town and went to the Moab Diner, hoping that Isaiah would be there, but he wasn't. He was spoiling for a fight. He thought he just might drive out to the man's ranch and confront him there, but doing so could very well get him shot.

Instead, Silas ate supper and then drove to the Red Rock Canyon Bookstore and stepped inside. If he couldn't confront the man directly, he'd do so electronically. He flicked the window-mounted air conditioner on and sat down in his chair. He took a can of beer from the tiny fridge and started to scan the web for stories about C. Thorn Smith's relationship with Isaiah, Barry, and Love. He spent an hour hunched over his aging desktop computer, clicking through online archives of environmental organizations, newspapers, and the US Senate.

Tired, his eyes starting to blur, he sat up and stretched, his shoulders popping. He leaned back in his chair and looked around the store. The muted lighting in the old adobe building cast a soft glow over his books. The rumble of a muffler on the road caught his attention; he looked from the far end of the narrow store to the single front window and scanned his collection as he did. He shook his head. Selling his own books as a pretext for being in Moab seemed absurd now. But the store had given him something to do when he wasn't searching for Penelope, and gave him an air of credibility in the tourist town.

He returned to his reading. There were a dozen stories about the senator's interest in business dealings in the Escalante region. He had supported the opening of the Monument to expanded oil and gas development, including hydraulic fracking. He had championed logging on the Kaiparowits Plateau. He had backed a plan to straighten and pave the winding Hole in the Rock Road to accommodate more tourists on the route. Silas dug back further into the archives of the *Salt Lake Tribune*. In a story, nearly seven years old, he found what he was looking for: the first mention of Senator Smith and the Glen Canyon Dam. The story had been written during the debate over refilling the reservoir behind the dam. At the time, Smith had been aggressively encouraging Congress to reconsider the Colorado River Compact.

Smith, it appeared, had been drafting an amendment to the Compact that would allow the upper basin states—Utah, Colorado, and Wyoming—to hold back more water behind the dividing line with the lower basin states. That dividing line was the Glen Canyon

Dam. If passed by both Houses of Congress, and signed by the Republican president at the time, the changes would have refilled Glen Canyon Dam, once again drowning the region's temples, buttes, and grottos under the silt-laden water.

It would have left the lower basin states of Arizona, Nevada, and California, as well as Mexico, high and dry. It would have been a second death for Glen Canyon, and places like the Grand Canyon, downstream, would have suffered dearly for a lack of water.

Penelope would have been devastated. She would have fought this with all of her heart and soul. So would Darcy McFarland and Kiel Pearce. So would Hayduke.

Silas sat back in his chair. His can of beer was empty. He took another from the fridge, opened it, and read the story again. He scanned the *Tribune* website for follow-up stories. There was one about the bill being introduced into a lame-duck session of Congress, but then nothing. Silas went to the website of the Senate of the United States and tried to find further mention of the legislation, but there was no mention of the bill after its introduction over five years ago. Silas couldn't find any mention of Barry, Isaiah, or Love in any of these articles.

For some reason, C. Thorn Smith had let the legislation drop and, when he did, the water in Lake Powell had done the same.

"SILAS."

He was dreaming. His wife was there.

"Silas. Wake up."

He didn't want to.

"Silas, the flames spread explosively. Wake up!"

WHEN SILAS TORE himself from sleep he had his head down on the desk at the back of the Red Rock Canyon Bookstore. The line from *Desert Solitaire* was etched in his mind. He had just reread them the night before in the chapter on Glen Canyon, now the focal point of his investigation. *The flames spread explosively*; Abbey had accidently started a brush fire in a side canyon and nearly been burned alive.

His first thought was *Please, not another body*. The side canyon that Abbey had described was now under the stagnant waters of Lake Powell.

Silas heard the sound of the ragged muffler on the road. Blearily he looked toward the front window again. *Some neighbor needs a new exhaust system*, he thought. There was a crash at the front of the store; the narrow building's single front window, next to the deeply inset door, shattered and a stone crashed into the center column of books. Silas jumped to his feet, knocking his desk, sending papers and the can of beer careening to the floor. He was halfway to the front of the store in a few long strides; the front window was shattered and the offending stone—a rock the size of a grapefruit—was on the floor. He looked up in time to see a figure on the street, illuminated by flames. The dark shape reared back with one hand and threw a burning Molotov cocktail through the broken window. Silas had to jump back to avoid being hit. The bottle collided with the front bookshelf and exploded, flames quickly engulfing the front of the building.

Silas tripped over the stone and landed on his back, pushing with his feet to get clear of the flames. His pants had small spots of fire on them where the gasoline from the homemade bomb had splashed on him. He patted them out with his hands. The fire rose up the bookshelves quickly, consuming the front of the store, blocking his only exit. Silas could see the doorway that led to the street through the raging fire but he couldn't reach it. He scrambled to his feet and ran for the back of the store. His cell phone was in his bag; he took it out and frantically dialed 911. The flames were rising up the walls and crossing the ancient log beams that held the adobe structure in place. Books burst as the fire consumed them.

Silas yelled over the din of the conflagration his address and that he was trapped. When the heat became too much, he dropped his phone and retreated to where the window-mounted air conditioner still sputtered. He looked back. The fire was halfway down the narrow building, the sound almost deafening. The flames created a wind tunnel, sucking the oxygen out of the room. As he stared at them, the flames seemed like an angry mouth that was consuming his world. He could feel the heat searing his face and his hands; his clothing felt as if they might burst into flames themselves. His eyes felt hot and he closed them for fear that they might melt.

He was trapped. There was no way out. He couldn't reach the door and it was the only exit. The air conditioner groaned to a halt as the power supply to the building was cut.

He pulled the desk to the edge of the window, the computer crashing to the floor. The AC unit was secured to the frame of the small window with heavy bolts. Pushing everything else off the table, he climbed onto it and lay on his back. With all his might, he kicked at the air conditioner. He could feel the flames closing in on him, smell the acrid reek of burning timbers and scorched clay brick. He kicked again and the AC unit budged. The ancient wood that held the screws fast began to split. He kicked and kicked and a voice rose up inside of him, furious and full of rage. He screamed as he kicked, the red hot air searing his throat. The wood frame of the window shattered and the unit was dislodged. He kicked again and it plunged out of the splintered frame and onto the ground. The open window allowed a rush of air to enter the burning building, feeding the flames. Silas pushed himself off the table, throwing it to the side, into the inferno. He dove for the window as the flames engulfed the rear of the building.

22

THERE WERE VOICES AND SIRENS all around him. Someone pulled him up off the dirt behind the store and half-carried him onto the street. He turned to watch the cottonwood tree that stretched over his store burst into a candelabra of flame. Branches and clots of dried leaves dripped like tears of fire onto the roofs of the homes and the street, setting both neighboring houses ablaze. He turned to see families rushing from their burning homes to join him. "Is everybody out?" he shouted over the roar of the flames.

The man next to him, a short Latino man, nodded and yelled yes. They all retreated across the street and watched their properties burn. Within minutes the road was clogged with all four of the Moab Valley Fire Department's fire trucks. A minute later, the seventy-five-foot aerial water vehicle was on scene, its ladder extended above the burning buildings, dousing the flames. Thick columns of steam and smoke rose into the night, obliterating the stars. Paramedics arrived, and the Grand County Sheriff's Department, and soon Silas was seated in the back of an ambulance. He could see Dexter Willis beyond the two paramedics who were working over his face, arms, and body. And beyond Willis were the still-blazing remains of the Red Rock Canyon Bookstore.

THE SUN WAS rising when the final flames were extinguished. All three buildings had collapsed as their log infrastructure was burned; the adobe now lay in smoldering piles. The cottonwood that had lived for a hundred and fifty years, sucking water from deep beneath the red sand, was gone. Three vehicles, including Silas's Outback, had burned beyond recognition.

Silas was wrapped in a blanket, his face red as if he'd been sunburned. His hair, normally as bristled as a hedgehog, was singed and looked like a wire brush. There was an oxygen mask around his neck but he had stopped sucking on the air sometime in the last hour. His throat felt raw, as if he'd swallowed sand. Someone had given him a cup of coffee, but he hadn't taken a drink; he held the cup in his hand, the contents now cold.

"Silas." It was Dexter Willis. "Silas, you alright?"

Silas looked up at him. "Not so well, Dex."

"I need to ask you a few questions. You okay with that?"

Silas nodded.

"Tell me what happened."

Silas told him about falling asleep, and waking to the sound of the rock being thrown through the window, and then seeing a figure throw the Molotov cocktail through the opening.

"Did you recognize this person?"

"No, it was dark. There's no streetlight out there. There was some light from the flames, but I couldn't make out any features."

"Man or woman?"

"I think it was a man. Just by the way he moved."

"Could you make out any clothing?"

"I think he was wearing a toque . . . a wool hat, like a longshoreman's cap. But it could have been anything."

"What about on the street? Did you see any vehicles that didn't belong?"

"I don't think so, Dex. It was only a split second."

"You're alright?"

"Feels like I've got one hell of a sunburn, and my throat feels like it's still on fire, but otherwise, I think I'm okay. A few burns on my hands. The fire was so hot that there wasn't much smoke in the building, so I got off easy. Wish I could say the same for the store."

"What did you lose?"

"Just every book I've ever collected. About seven thousand titles."

"They were yours? Your own collection?"

"Yeah, mine and Penelope's."

"The fire inspector is going to want to talk with you. And I guess you'll have to call your insurance people if they aren't already here. Do you need anything?"

"*Another* new car."

23

HE MADE THE CALLS FROM a phone at the municipal building.

"Katie, it's Silas."

"Oh Silas, are you alright? What happened?"

"Someone firebombed my store, with me in it. I'm at the Grand County municipal office. I've got a sit-down with the fire inspector coming up."

"Were you hurt?"

"A little charred here and there. Might need some aloe. Otherwise, fine. Burned my shirt right off me but left me pretty much intact."

"Did you see who did it?"

"No. Just a shape, a man. He seemed stiff, like maybe he had arthritis."

"You think you know who did this, don't you."

"I have my suspicions."

"Taylor knows what's going on. He's on his way into Moab right now. He thinks this is tied to the investigation into Penelope."

"So do I."

"Don't hold out on him, Silas. He can help."

"Where are you?"

"Salt Lake."

"Robbie is there. He got in late last night. He called to say he was staying at the Holiday Inn downtown."

"Give me his cell number and I'll show him the town."

"What are you going to do, buy him a hot chocolate?"

"DAD, ARE YOU alright?"

"Yeah, I'm fine. What about you?"

"I'm good. Do you want me to come back to Moab?"

"So you can what? Take care of me? I'm okay. A little singed. You should see my hair. No, don't come back. But listen, Robbie, I want you to change hotels, alright?"

"Dad, seriously?"

"Just do it, alright, for me? And Katie Rain is going to call you."

"The FBI agent? Cool—she's really hot."

"HOLY SWEET MOTHERFUCKER, are you alright?"

"Yeah, I'm fine. What about you?"

"Yeah, I'm good. I just got in from the mountains and heard the news."

"Where are you?"

"I'm over at Back of Beyond Books. Hanging out in the Abbey section."

"Watch your back, Hayduke. I think whoever came after me knows about you, and what we're doing."

"What *are* we doing?"

"We're nailing someone's ass to the wall."

"Wow, you swore! You must be pissed."

"Pissed doesn't start to describe what I'm feeling."

"DR. PEARSON, HOW are you holding up?"

"Well, I think I should get some sleep sometime soon."

"This will just take a minute. Can we get you anything?"

"A glass of water. I'm feeling a little parched."

"Eugene, would you mind? So, I've been briefed by Sheriff Willis and the fire inspector. They've recovered fragments of the glass from the incendiary device from your store, but I doubt they are going to be much help. I don't think our lab will be able to lift any fingerprints or DNA. That's the bad news. The good news is we might have tire-tread marks. There was a set of pretty fresh tracks on the road about fifty yards from the store. They were messed up by all the emergency vehicles and footprints, but it's a start. We've also got two video surveillance cameras in town that might have picked something up. Grand County sheriff's deputies are requesting footage for review."

"Here's your water, Dr. Pearson."

"Thank you, Agent Nielsen."

"Dr. Pearson, can you tell us anything else that you remember from last night?"

"I heard a car go by right before. I heard one a little earlier too."

"That could be helpful."

"And, of course, I saw the guy."

"What can you tell us?"

"Male, I think, but it's hard to tell if he was young or old. He wasn't as fluid as I thought a young man would be. A little stiff; arthritic."

"Black, white, Hispanic?"

"I don't know. I think white, but only because I would imagine a black person would be obvious in the dim light."

"Maybe, maybe not. I'm as black as it gets in these parts; I'm not sure if I was wearing a hat and in the middle of a dark street you'd know I was African-American. You said to Sheriff Willis you thought the assailant was wearing a wool cap?"

"That's right. And a coat. He had a coat on. I remember that because it was ungodly hot, even before the fire, and I wondered why he was wearing a coat."

"Can you tell us if you've had any recent altercations that might lead anyone to want to try to kill you?"

"It's funny, until you said it just now, I hadn't really thought of it that way. I just thought someone was trying to send me a message; you know, burn down my store."

"They knew you were in there. Your lights were on. Your car was out front. Can you think of anyone?"

"I don't know if I should talk about this."

"You can't be a suspect in an attempt on your own life."

"That's not what I mean. Agent Nielsen here recently threatened to put me in jail and ship me back to Canada if I interfered with your investigation into Penelope's death. I take that sort of thing seriously."

"Not seriously enough, obviously."

"Eugene, it's alright. Listen, Dr. Pearson, Agent Nielsen has a job to do. So do I. We can't have you tripping up our investigation. But this is important. If you tell us who you've been rattling, we'll let it go, but just this time."

"I've got your word?"

"You've got our word."

24

SPECIAL AGENT TAYLOR WALKED SILAS to the door of the municipal offices. "What now, Dr. Pearson?"

"It's funny; everybody wants to know what I'm going to do next, as if I have some plan."

"Don't you?"

"My plan is to get a haircut. My head smells like a dead animal left in a campfire. I'm going to buy some clothing. Get a new cell phone. And then I'm going to rent a car. Maybe a truck. After that, who knows?"

"Our deal won't cover you if you continue to investigate and get in our way; you know that, right?"

"Don't worry, Agent Taylor, I'll behave."

AFTER RUNNING HIS errands, Silas ate breakfast at the Moab Diner, where it didn't matter as much if he still smelled like a fire. He drove home and was relieved when he pulled into the driveway that his house was still standing.

He parked and quickly assembled his gear, loading it into the back of the rented SUV. He went to the bedroom last, throwing some clothing into a bag, and then opened the hiding place in his closet where he kept Penelope's journal. It wasn't there.

Silas stopped cold. Since discovering the journal the previous summer, he'd always guarded it closely. He took it with him on some of his trips, but most of the time, in an effort to keep it safe and secret, he stashed it in this hiding place. Nobody else knew where it was. Not even Robbie.

He searched the house, which didn't take long. Even though he'd lived there for more than four years, the house was nearly empty. The journal was nowhere to be found. Had he taken it with him to Moab the night before? If he had, it would be cinders too, burned up in the car or the bookstore. But he knew he hadn't. Someone had broken into his house and stolen the journal. How would they have known where to look? Nothing else had been taken. The thief knew what they were looking for. Whoever had done this was likely the same person who tried to kill him. What was the connection between the journal and burning his store? Was there something in that journal he had overlooked? Silas knew in his heart that he'd never have the chance to check; it was gone, and with it one of his last links to his wife.

He *should* call Dexter Willis and report the break-in. Maybe the perpetrator had left fingerprints. But he had never told Willis or Agent Taylor about the journal, and to do so now would raise many uncomfortable questions, and open him to further interrogation and accusations about obstruction of justice. And, Silas reasoned, the thief had likely worn gloves anyway.

He showered quickly, washing the last of the smoke and soot from himself. After putting on his new clothes, he left the house, locking the door behind him.

HE DROVE AS far Goblin Valley State Park, where fatigue overtook him. He pulled off the highway and rented a campsite, and fell into a restless sleep, plagued by claustrophobic nightmares about being trapped in ancient ruins, in a mine shaft, in a burning bookstore, while the world around him turned to ash.

THE ESCALANTE'S BROAD plateau was compressed beneath a sky dark with thunderheads. Silas arrived before noon the following day. Almost immediately after driving into town he came upon Hayduke's gunmetal-blue Jeep, parked near the now-familiar pizza parlor.

He parked his Explorer nearby and walked into the restaurant.

Hayduke was his usual theatrical self, jumping to his feet and embracing Silas in a bear hug. "Holy shit, am I glad to see you!"

"Thanks, it's good to see you too."

They ordered pizza and Hayduke ordered a pitcher of beer, and they sat in the quiet restaurant comparing notes from the last couple of days. Hayduke was beside himself with grief that the prized journal had gone missing, but quickly rebounded. "We got to get on with the show," he offered as encouragement.

As noon approached the restaurant began to fill up. Soon most of the tables around them were filled with locals or tourists. As the pair finished their meal, Eleanor Barry walked into the restaurant with two men. She immediately saw Silas, and he thought she might turn around and walk back out, but in an obvious act of defiance, she sat down at a table on the other side of the room.

"What is it?" asked Hayduke.

"Eleanor Barry just walked in."

"No fucking shit."

"Josh, I don't want a scene."

"Hey, man, I'm not the one who just had his place burned to the ground by these fuckers."

"Not now."

"When?" Hayduke stood up, brushing crumbs from his beard and lap onto the table.

Silas reached for him but the young man was already approaching the Barry table.

The exchange was clearly audible over the din of the room. "You're Eleanor Barry?" said Hayduke, extending a hand.

Barry tentatively shook it. "We've met before, haven't we?"

"I don't know, maybe. Who's this?"

"My husband, Frank, and one of our friends, Mac."

"Nice to meet you folks. My friend Silas and I are just back in town trying to figure out who killed his wife." Several people in the restaurant turned to look at Hayduke now. He was swaying back and forth with nervous energy.

"Mr. . . ."

"Name's Hayduke."

"Mr. Hayduke, we're just having a quick lunch. I don't think this is the time or the place—"

"Sure it is! That man right there, his wife was killed out there in the desert. She was my friend. She had just put the brakes on your big development scheme, and then she gets killed a few miles from where you wanted to build your resort. Tell me that's a coincidence!"

Silas was on his feet, as was Frank Barry. Silas got a hand on Hayduke's shoulder and said, "Come on, not now."

Hayduke shrugged him off. "And then one of you fuckers burned down his bookstore, with him in it. Was it you?" he roared.

"You're going to have to leave," said Frank Barry, calmly. He was a large man, heavy across the middle, but clearly powerful.

"Come on, Hayduke." Silas reached for the young man again.

"No, I'm sick and tired of this. You people think that because you've got money and connections you can get away with murder! Well, not this time."

Frank Barry stepped in front of Hayduke as if to guide him out of the restaurant, but Hayduke would have none of it. He swung for Barry's head, his punch forming a compact arc, like a practiced boxer. Barry managed to lean back enough that the blow just glanced his chin. People in the restaurant gasped. Mac was on his feet quickly and tackled Hayduke before he could swing a second time. The two men landed hard on the floor, sending chairs scattering around the restaurant. Frank and Mac got Hayduke to his feet and with powerful arms muscled him to the door and threw him out.

Silas was left standing in the restaurant. His eyes locked with Eleanor Barry's for a moment; he tried to read an expression of guilt there, but couldn't find anything. Silas turned and left. He had to walk past Mac and Frank, who were standing, arms crossed, at the door, waiting—hoping?—that Hayduke would try and return.

THE SINGLE GARFIELD County sheriff's deputy stationed in Escalante arrived within five minutes. Silas and Hayduke were still standing on the street near Silas's Explorer, arguing, when the patrol vehicle pulled up next to them.

Hayduke looked at Silas, and then around at his options. The deputy got out of his SUV, placed a cap on his head, and with his hand on the butt of his sidearm, approached.

"Step away from the vehicle," the deputy ordered. "Put your hands behind your head."

Silas did as he was told. Hayduke hesitated. "Do it now, sir."

Hayduke, exasperated and clearly disgusted, complied. The deputy searched him and then explained that he was being arrested. He cuffed Hayduke's wrists behind his back and led him to the waiting patrol vehicle. Silas lowered his hands. His eyes locked with Hayduke's and he watched the young man be loaded into the back of the car. Then the street was empty again and Silas stood alone on the sidewalk.

25

ROBBIE PEARSON STOOD IN FRONT of the BLM office just off the interstate in Salt Lake City. In a few minutes he was seated at a small table in a brightly lit room with a thick file folder in front of him and several tubes of maps.

"Let me know if you need anything," the man who had escorted him into the room said before closing the door.

He spent two hours there, poring over the proposal for the Escalante Resort. He found plenty of reasons why Penelope would have opposed it, but little to indicate any corroboration between Senator Smith and Eleanor Barry, Paul Love, or Jacob Isaiah.

He was getting ready to pack it in when his cell phone rang. It was his father.

"I forgot to tell you the other day," said Silas. "Before the fire at the store, I was doing some digging into Smith."

"Yeah, I'm doing the same at the BLM. I'm looking at the Escalante Resort application and environmental impact statement right now. I'm not finding anything new."

"What's the date on the application?"

Robbie told him.

"You see, that's too late. Something happened before that and

Smith stopped talking about Glen Canyon, Lake Powell, and the Colorado River Compact."

"So Smith had legislation about the Compact before the Senate, and then he let it die? Why would he do that?"

"That's what we need to find out."

"I'm not seeing it in the records at the BLM office. But I've got an idea."

"Oh, by the way, Hayduke has been arrested. He got in a fight in the pizza parlor in Escalante." Silas told him what happened.

"You going to bail him out?"

"I don't know. He's being held in Panguitch, which is an hour and a half away. He's being formally charged tomorrow morning."

"You should go and post for him."

"Why?"

"Because if you don't, there's going to be trouble. Plus, he's bailed you out a few times. I might not like him, but he's been there for you. You need to be there for him."

"I'VE BEEN COVERING Utah politics since Brigham Young was the Governor of Utah."

"When was that?"

"1851."

Robbie laughed and bought the man a cup of coffee. "I appreciate you seeing me, Mr. Dawson."

"It's just James. Or Jim. You've got some interesting questions, and while I'm old, I'm not out to pasture yet. I still keep a desk at the *Tribune*, and I can write pretty much anything I want. I'll tell you what I know, and if anything you've got going leads to a story, I'd like first crack at it. Agreed?"

Robbie nodded and sat down by the window of the café. Jim Dawson sat across from him. He fidgeted as if he wanted a cigarette. "So, what do you want to know?"

"Tell me about C. Thorn Smith."

Dawson smiled. "What's he done *now*?"

"Somehow he's involved in a project to develop a resort in the Escalante region. My father's wife was trying to stop the resort, and she did, at least temporarily. But then she disappeared, and she was recently—"

"Found. Yes, of course. De Silva, right?"

"That's right. Penelope de Silva. She went missing five years ago. Her body wasn't found until recently. My father, her husband, moved to Moab to be closer to where he thought she disappeared. He has been searching—"

"Searching for her ever since. Yes, yes, I cover politics, but everybody in the press knows about your father. We call him the Dreamer."

"I know. He *loves* that."

"What does C. Thorn have to do with this?"

"I was hoping *you* would tell me. He was a backer of this project, a booster I guess you'd call it. But suddenly he dropped off the radar screen." Robbie filled him in on the possible connection between the Escalante Resort and Penelope's murder.

"Yes, of course. Now I get it. Did he drop off the radar screen before or after Ms. de Silva was murdered?"

"Before. But not by much. A few months or so."

"And this project, it was in the Escalante?"

Robbie told him about the project and its backers.

"Of course, don't you see? These people are all connected, at least the major players. Eleanor Barry was C. Thorn Smith's executive assistant when he was mayor of Salt Lake City. She was with him on his gubernatorial campaign, and served under him for both his terms here. There were rumors, gossip really, that she actually did serve *under* him, if you know what I mean. But that was never proven."

"She is the face of this project. She runs a real estate development business out of Escalante now. And she's got Jacob Isaiah as a major backer."

"You see, there's another connection. Isaiah has had his hand in the senator's pocket since Smith's first term as governor. Isaiah has funded both of Smith's gubernatorial campaigns, as well as his various runs for the US Senate."

"So it's easy to see why Smith would back the Escalante project."

"Of course, but he backs every development opportunity that comes along. He's never met a mine, a gas field, a hydro project, or a resort scheme that he didn't like. It's his Achilles heel. It works well in Utah, but it doesn't play well outside of the West. Voters in Utah love his boosterism, but it doesn't do him much good in Iowa, New Hampshire, or South Carolina."

"The first three US presidential primaries. But being too tight with the business community can't hurt you *that* much, can it? Didn't you have a vice president who ran a major oil services company out of the White House recently?"

Dawson laughed. "So true. No, it's just that Smith has more challenging blind spots."

"What's the dirt on him?"

"Well, it may have started with Eleanor Barry, but I don't think it ended there."

"But you've had presidents who have been philanderers in the past."

"True, true, but I think someone has something particularly incriminating on Thorn, and they are lording it over him."

"Do you know who?"

"No idea. If I did, I'd have put the thumbscrews to them."

It was Robbie's turn to laugh. "My dad thinks that the senator is mixed up in Penelope's death somehow."

"It's not out of the question, but it's a hell of a stretch. She was a thorn in his side, if you'll pardon the pun. I could see him taking someone out politically, digging up some particularly incriminating opposition research, but I don't see him killing someone."

"He proposed amendments to the Colorado River Compact a few years back. Then he dropped them. What was that about?"

"He wanted more water for the upper basin states. But California, Arizona, and New Mexico have more electoral college votes and have more members in the House of Representatives; it was a no-win situation. He had to let it drop."

"There wasn't something else? What about this rumored dirt?"

"I haven't heard of anything." Dawson made a note in his pocket notebook for the first time during the conversation. "But let me look into it."

"Will you call me if you find anything?"

"You bet. You know, it's a funny thing about Smith. He's got something up his sleeve. He's a climber. Mayor, governor, senator. What's next? He's a young man, just early sixties; he's got a lot of political life left in him. If someone really does have dirt on him, and it was bad enough that it would keep him from the next rung on the ladder—a long-shot run for the party nomination, say, and maybe the second billing on the big ticket—then I might reconsider what I just said. That might be enough to push him over the edge."

26

SILAS DROVE TO PANGUITCH THE following morning. In the middle of October, the weather in the high plateau of southwestern Utah could fluctuate wildly from brilliant sunshine to violent storms. Silas got a little of both on his hour-and-a-half drive. A brief deluge near Bryce Canyon forced him off the road until the sun appeared and cast golden light across the storybook landscape.

He arrived in the small town set in a green valley between upland portions of the Dixie National Forest an hour before Hayduke's scheduled court appearance. He ate breakfast at a diner on Main Street and proceeded to the courthouse.

Shortly after he arrived, Hayduke's case was called. The young man was led into the courtroom wearing a jumpsuit emblazoned with the words GARFIELD COUNTY SHERIFF'S DEPARTMENT. He looked pale and disheveled.

The case docket was read and a public defender made a brief statement explaining that the situation had been an innocent dispute and that Mr. Charleston had promised to apologize to the complainants to settle the matter out of court. He asked that the Class B misdemeanor charges be dropped.

The prosecutor rose to her feet and explained that Mr. Charleston had a history of violent behavior, had been charged with assault in the past, and had recently spent several months under close supervision for both physical and mental trauma associated with post-traumatic stress disorder.

"This young man," said the prosecutor, "has a troubling propensity for aggression and antisocial behavior. He has no ties to Garfield County and is a flight risk before trial. The people recommend bail be set at twenty-five thousand dollars."

Hayduke looked straight ahead. From behind, in the gallery, Silas couldn't discern the expression on his face.

The public defender spoke briefly with Hayduke. The young man nodded and then the public defender addressed the court. "My client is a veteran of the Second Gulf War, your honor, and has undergone treatment for post-traumatic stress disorder in the past. After suffering an injury earlier this year, he voluntarily sought treatment for recurring trauma associated with his combat experience. He is not a threat to society. We suggest a more reasonable bail of one thousand dollars, which is more in keeping with charges associated with a simple scuffle."

The judge set the bail at five thousand dollars and Hayduke, without a glance back, disappeared from the courtroom, his head down.

SILAS WAS WAITING for him when he emerged from the court building.

"You alright?"

"Yeah, I'm fine." The young man sounded subdued.

"Josh—"

"It's nothing, Silas. I'm fine, really. Getting shot just triggered some stuff. Some bad feelings. I worked through them."

"Where were you?"

"Seattle, with my parents."

"I thought your complexion looked more West Coast than Baja."

"You bailed me out." It was a statement, not a question.

"Yes."

"Why did you do that?"

"I figure I owed you. Plus, I can't have my sidekick locked up in the joint. Who'd watch my back?"

"What are we going to do now?" asked Hayduke.

"What do you mean? We've got to get back to Escalante, man. We've got work to do!"

"AGENT TAYLOR, IT'S Silas Pearson." He was standing in the washroom of a gas station halfway between Panguitch and Escalante.

There was a moment's pause. "What can I do for you, Dr. Pearson?"

"In the spring, when we were in Page, you told me that my . . . acquaintance Josh Charleston had a criminal record."

"He does: assault."

"I just picked him up from a courtroom here in Garfield County. He got into it with Eleanor Barry's husband and ended up punching him."

"That sounds consistent with his impulsive behavior."

"I don't know how stable the man is. I wonder if you have people who could do a behavioral profile?"

"What does this have to do with the cases we are working on?"

"Likely nothing, Agent Taylor, but I'd feel a lot better if we could rule some things out. I'm starting to feel as if Mr. Charleston is more liability than benefit to this . . ."

"You were going to say investigation, but then you know that you're supposed to be keeping your nose out of this, don't you?"

"I'm thinking that Josh might be doing more harm than good."

"I'd say that is true for both of you, Dr. Pearson, but yes, maybe more so for your friend *Hayduke*."

"IT'S A TOWN of eight hundred people; I don't think you'll just blend in."

"If my Jeep hasn't been towed, just drop me there. I'll camp out in the Monument; I'm happier that way anyway." Hayduke had been mostly quiet for the hour-and-a-half drive back to Escalante.

They drove into town and Hayduke's Jeep was where he had left it. As Hayduke was getting out of the rental he stopped. "You know, this shit doesn't make any sense. Your good buddy Jacob Isaiah, and that fucker who pointed a gun at us, Paul Love—I just don't see how they could have killed all those people."

"I do. I think it's perfectly feasible. They had a lot of money on the line."

"They had money on the line in the Hatch Canyon business, and at the Grand Canyon, but in the end, neither of them was involved in the death of the Wisechild girl or your wife's friend from Flag."

"They were involved, but just not in the way we thought. What are you thinking?"

"You told me that Smith's name has come up again." Hayduke had his hand on the frame of the Ford but hadn't gotten out.

"Yeah; he had this big idea a bunch of years back to rewrite the Colorado River Compact. Hold more water behind Glen Canyon Dam for the upper basin states. Surely you and Penelope must have discussed this."

"A little, but that sort of thing, you know, legislation and such, didn't interest me much. I'm more of an action kind of guy. So, you think the Compact ties into what Eleanor Barry wants?"

"I do. Both she and her investors want the water level high enough to build a new marina at the Hole in the Rock. It's not going to happen unless we can reverse climate change or find some other way of refilling Lake Powell."

Hayduke said, "I think this all comes back to Smith. He's been a constant throughout all of this. That slimy fucker wanted to refill Lake Powell by changing the Law of the River six or seven years ago. I bet if that kid of yours looks into it, he'll find out that C. Thorn is back at it again. Didn't you tell me he's touring around the state talking about water?"

"That's right. I saw him in Blanding the other day. But why now?"

"Because everybody who was trying to stop him is dead."

"You're not."

Hayduke straightened up and looked around. "Not yet."

27

"IT'S JIM DAWSON CALLING. I wonder if you've got a minute this morning to have coffee?"

Twenty minutes later Robbie Pearson was sitting in a coffee shop a few blocks east of the *Salt Lake Tribune* offices. Dawson was waiting for him.

"You said this might be important?" Robbie sat down with a coffee.

"It might be. I don't know." Dawson drew a deep breath. "Six years ago, one of my colleagues—a veteran political reporter named Harvey Kresge—died in a car accident. He was on his way to cover a rally in Price and he went over the guardrail on Soldier Summit. There wasn't much left of him or his car. They say his brakes failed. Whatever happened, Kresge was working on a lot of files at the time. This was just before C. Thorn's last run for reelection for the Senate and old Harvey was the bulldog assigned to cover him. Now, don't get me wrong here; the paper had endorsed Smith. They were big fans. But Harvey marched to his own drummer, and he wasn't making it easy for Smith. So, tragic accident. And nobody really picked things up. All his files got put in the basement and that was that. Kresge had this habit of holding all his sources close to his chest. He'd written *Personal, do not open* on the boxes of his paper files, so nobody had. After our conversation the other day, I decided to go and have a look. I remembered that Kresge had done a few stories on this Colorado River Compact business and wanted to see what he might have had.

"I spent a few hours reading his notes. Your stepmother was a royal pain in the ass to C. Thorn Smith. I mean, Kresge had a whole file filled with information that she had provided him. None of it had ever been used in print, but it was damning stuff."

"What was it? No, wait, don't tell me. Smith was having an affair. The rumors were true."

"There were photos."

"You're kidding. And Penelope was the one that had these? Jesus, I never thought that Penelope would play that kind of hardball."

"She was, and she did."

"And she gave all this to Kresge?"

"She did. I don't think she took the photos herself. I don't know who did. They were in a file that Kresge had with Penelope's name on them. It looks like private eye stuff. No nudes or anything, thank God, but there were shots of Eleanor Barry holding hands with the senator and him looking all dewy-eyed at her. There was one of them kissing. It looks like it was shot through the back window of a car. Both of them were married to other people at the time."

Robbie was quiet for a while. Dawson sipped his coffee. Finally Robbie spoke. "You think that Penelope gave these same photos to the senator?"

"Not much good to her or her cause if she didn't."

"So my father's wife was blackmailing a US senator."

"Risky business, son. Very high-risk proposition. And there's more. There was a purpose to this blackmail. It wasn't about money. It was about something that seemed way more important to Ms. de Silva."

"The Colorado River."

"You got it. The Compact. I figure she struck a deal with Kresge. She was feeding him stories, and gave him the photos to hold on to. I think the deal was that if Smith didn't drop the senate bill to amend the Colorado River Compact, then he could publish them."

"Why wouldn't Kresge just publish them anyway? What was in it for him to hold onto a juicy story just so some environmentalist could kill a bill in the Senate?"

"Good question. I can't be sure. De Silva must have had something else for Kresge; otherwise he would have run them leading up to the election six years ago."

"You haven't found out what that was?"

"Not yet. I'm going to dig further. But I think I can guess."

"No way. That wasn't her—"

"Easy, son, that's not what I meant. I think she offered him exclusivity. There's got to be more copies of these images kicking around. Someone must be holding a copy of them. There were other names in the files, people that Kresge talked to, or who were helping him dig up dirt on the Colorado Compact story. Wanna guess who?"

Robbie didn't hesitate. "Darcy McFarland."

The reporter held up his index finger indicating that was one.

"Kiel Pearce."

A second finger. Robbie felt his stomach turn over.

"Two more names. I don't think that Kresge ever talked to them. I'm not really sure who they are. One guy's name is Josh Charleston."

Robbie's mind was racing. His hands had started to sweat and he rubbed them on his jeans until they were hot. "Hayduke. He calls himself Hayduke."

"Abbey fan, hey? Get a lot of those in the environmental biz. The other guy's name was Tabby Dingwall."

"Hayduke—Josh—knew Penelope; he helped her out with her work to protect the Southwest. My dad knows him."

"And Dingwall?"

"Never heard of him."

"Well, somehow they were all listed in this file that Kresge had on the Compact. They were all tied together somehow. Pearce, McFarland, and de Silva are all dead. Three people who were blackmailing a sitting US senator, one with his eye on the big ticket, have all been murdered, their bodies found within a stone's throw of the Colorado River. All wanted to kill a bill that the same US senator was trying to move through Congress."

"And that same senator is now starting to talk about water again, just a few weeks after Penelope's body has been found. Out of curiosity, did you find anything in that file about Jacob Isaiah?"

"One thing. A letter. It was just a handwritten note, really. It looked like someone had made a photocopy. It said something to the effect of *Keep your promise to refill Lake Powell or it won't be the only thing that dries up.*"

"Wow, everybody was blackmailing Smith—his enemies and his friends."

"I guess the question is: Was this past tense, or present? Three of the people with the goods on Smith's penis problems are dead, but you say this Josh Charleston is still in play, and we don't know about Tabby Dingwall. And Jacob Isaiah is still alive and kicking, as are Barry and Love. So if all these people were blackmailing him then, who is still blackmailing him now?" asked the reporter.

"And if they are, was this something that he'd be willing to kill for?"

"I'm going to have to go and talk with our crime reporters about this. Like I said, we've all heard of your father, but I do politics, so I haven't really paid too much attention to this angle. You know I'm going to want to write about this."

"I figured you'd want to. I can't stop you. I don't have anything to offer. But can I ask you for a favor?"

"You mean *another* favor? Why not?"

"Wait. Just give my dad and me a week or so to try and use what we've got here and figure things out. Let me see if I can find any remaining photos, or whatever might be linked to this Colorado River story, and when I do, you've got the exclusive."

"Same deal as Kresge."

"Same deal."

"But he's dead."

"That seems to be the theme here."

"HEY DAD, IT'S Robbie. I guess you're out of cell phone range right now. Listen, I just talked with that reporter from the *Tribune* again. You better call me. I think Senator Smith is mixed up in Penelope's murder in a *big* way. It turns out he was, well, having an affair with Eleanor Barry and there were photos. I think Penelope, Kiel, Darcy, and maybe even Josh were blackmailing the senator in order to kill his Colorado River Compact bill. There's more too. The reporter, the one who Penelope gave the original photos to, *he* was killed. Brakes failed. Sound familiar? I think Smith is dangerous, Dad. Oh, and there is another name that came up: Tabby Dingwall? According to the reporter, this guy knew Penelope. Keep a watch out for that name. Anyway, call me."

28

HAYDUKE APPEARED THE NEXT MORNING while Silas was eating breakfast at a small café on Main Street. Silas looked around to see if anybody else noticed him slip into the booth.

"What's with the sunglasses?" asked Silas.

"I'm trying to go incognito."

"You should shave and get a haircut then."

"No way, man. This is my identity." Hayduke pretended to groom his beard. Something fell out of it onto the table. "Bet you wonder why I'm here." Silas nodded, finishing his breakfast. "C. Thorn Smith. The senior senator for the great state of Utah will be in Boulder this afternoon. He's holding a series of town hall meetings."

"The same thing as in Blanding?"

"What else? The total destruction of the American Southwest." Hayduke read from a printed page of text. "*The Colorado River: Restoring the Promise of Water Security.* This is what Penelope was fighting, Silas. This is what she died for."

"You don't know that."

"Wake up, man! The guy who is responsible for your wife's murder is going to be just down the road this afternoon. I think you might want to go ask him a few questions."

IT WAS AGREED that Hayduke would not attend the town hall meeting.

"You're afraid I'll rock the boat, stir up the shit!"

"I'm afraid you'll get arrested and get *me* thrown in jail with you."

Silas drove north along the Hogsback, a narrow spine of rock with a two-lane highway laid down along its convoluted summit. The views from the road were dazzling, the vast expanse of the Escalante National Monument stretched out to the edge of the horizon. In the distance a collision of cumulus clouds was producing cloud-to-cloud lightning, the flashes coming every few seconds, while below the red earth was stippled in the perfect light of autumn.

As Silas drove he considered the town hall meeting in Boulder. What had prompted Senator Smith to restart discussions on refilling Lake Powell now? If this had been what Penelope had been fighting before she disappeared and was murdered, was the discovery of her remains somehow tied to the senator's decision?

There was only one way to find out.

THE TOWN OF Boulder gave Escalante the air of a thriving metropolis. Its population of 180 hadn't changed much in over one hundred years. He quickly found the town library where the community meeting was being held. There were two dozen cars and pickup trucks, each dusted with red earth, parked around the community hub. Silas checked his watch; the meeting would begin in fifteen minutes. As he parked, his cell phone buzzed. His reception was bad. He listened for messages. Dwight Taylor had called him back. He quickly returned the call.

"Dr. Pearson, thanks for getting back to me."

Silas was walking around his rental in an effort to find the best cell signal. "I haven't got very good reception, Agent Taylor. What have you learned?"

"About what?"

"About Josh Charleston; isn't that why you called me back?"

"I'm afraid not. Where are you, Dr. Pearson?"

"I'm in Boulder. Why?"

"You're not by any chance there to talk with Senator Smith, are you?"

"How do you know that Senator Smith is in town?"

"Special Agent Nielsen happened to talk with Mr. Charleston in the last hour. Dr. Pearson, I think it would be in your best interest if you didn't confront Senator Smith this afternoon."

Silas had wandered into a dusty field adjacent to the library. "Are you investigating Senator Smith for the murder of my wife, Agent Taylor?"

"I am asking—and, if I have to, ordering you—to stay away from Smith."

"Ordering? I don't see how you can do that, Taylor." Silas was gritting his teeth as he spoke.

"I can ask the Garfield County Sheriff's Department to detain you for interfering in a federal investigation."

"So you *are* investigating Smith for Penny's murder."

Taylor's voice had a growing edge to it. "I am not saying that. Penelope de Silva's murder is not the only case that the FBI is investigating in this Field Unit. Now, I am asking you for the last time, do not interfere with our investigation. You need to leave Boulder."

"No way. I'm heading into the meeting right now." He hung up and noticed there was another message as he did. It was from Robbie.

THE TEMPERATURE IN the Boulder Library was in the eighties; the room was full when Silas stepped in and found a place to stand at the back.

After he was introduced, Smith said, "Thanks, everybody. I really appreciate you taking time out of your busy day to come and tell me what's on your mind. As you know, Washington is gridlocked over partisan feuding and the president isn't likely to demonstrate leadership on anything important to people outside of Hollywood or New York City. I've decided to spend some time with real folks, folks with character, good folks who remember what it means to be American."

The people applauded. "I want to hear from you today. What's important to you?"

"Lower taxes!" someone in the room shouted.

"The second amendment!"

"That's important to me too, friends. That's why I keep standing up in the Senate for Utah. I want to talk with you about something else that's important: water. We don't have much of it here in the West, and we don't have much of it in Utah. Nearly fifty years ago now, we spent a lot of time and money to build a dam that would help keep what little water we have in Utah from running off to Mexico and the Sea of Cortez. Those of us in the upper basin states agreed to allow a certain amount of water to continue on down to Arizona, Nevada, California, and to Mexico. Friends, that agreement isn't working anymore. Lake Powell is at its lowest level in twenty years, and what for? So Las Vegas can have fountains and California can grow avocados? Don't get me wrong; everybody should get to use their water however they want. But folks, Utah, along with Colorado and Wyoming, are getting a bum deal out of this. We need to fill up Lake Powell again, and we need to renegotiate our deal with the lower basin states so that we get our fair share. That way Utah can once again use our water to fuel our industry, tourism, and agriculture.

"Here's what I'd like to do: I want to bring forward a bill in the Senate that would mandate the Department of the Interior to renegotiate the Colorado River Compact. Did you know that this so-called Law of the River is coming up on one hundred years old? Can you believe that a deal written before any of us in this room were born is dictating what's what with Utah's water?

"Now, I'd like to hear from you."

A few hands went up from the fifty or so people gathered in the heat. The senator answered questions about taxes, big government, and gun control. One woman who owned a popular restaurant in town asked about incentives for tourism in the area.

"I'm glad you asked that. People come here to see the canyons and the desert. But that doesn't mean they don't want to enjoy the water as well. Houseboating on Lake Powell is still one of the most popular activities in this state. But that form of good clean family recreation is in trouble. If the environmentalists had their way, they'd drain Lake Powell and make it inaccessible to regular people once again. I don't want to let that happen. I want Lake Powell filled to the brim once more. And I'd like to see more access to the lake's magnificent waters; that's why I'm getting behind the plan to build a resort and marina at the end of the Hole in the Rock Road. I know that won't help Boulder as much as it would a resort along the Burr Trail, but we'll get one of these done and then I'll get behind another."

There were a few more questions from the group and then Silas couldn't hold back any longer. He raised his hand. The senator didn't seem to recognize him and called on him.

"Senator, I wonder if you might tell us why your first effort to pass this legislation failed?"

"Ah, Mr. Pearson, I didn't recognize you back there. Are you a resident of Boulder now?" A few ball-cap-wearing heads turned to look at Silas.

"I'm not. Just here to enjoy the scenery. One of those tourists you were talking about. Can you answer the question?"

"The Democrats in Congress wouldn't get behind my bill. So much for the spirit of bipartisanship!" Smith smiled congenially at the small group.

"But your bill never got to the floor of the Senate. As far as I can tell, neither the Democrats or Republicans got a chance to see it. Why did you kill your own bill? You would have had a better chance to pass it six years ago with a president from your own party."

A few people in the room turned and looked distastefully at Silas. At least one or two seemed to agree with his line of questioning.

"We did the calculus and decided that it just wasn't the time."

"And now it is? Why is that? Is it because six years ago someone *else* was threatening the bill?"

The county commissioner stepped next to the senator and spoke. "Alright, let's move on to the next question. Ted, I think you wanted to ask about agricultural subsidies, didn't you?"

Silas spoke over the commissioner. "Isn't it true that six years ago you had every intention of pushing your bill forward, but my wife and her friends—those environmentalists you seem to hate so much—had evidence that you were having an affair, and you pulled the bill to keep them quiet?"

The room's decibel level rose dramatically. Silas watched as people turned to one another. He heard an older man ask the woman sitting next to him, "Did he just say what I think he said?"

The commissioner took the microphone. "There's no call for that sort of accusation—"

Silas could see the senator's security moving toward him. Smith stood smiling at the front of the room; he was shaking his head in an almost apologetic way.

"There's proof. You thought you got rid of it all, didn't you? You thought you had cleaned up all the loose ends, but there's still proof." Silas wasn't shouting but in the small room his voice, edged with desperation, filled the space.

"Come with us, sir." Two men in suits were standing next to him now. One put a hand on his arm. Silas shook it off.

"What are you going to do, Senator? Have *me* killed *too*?"

The room was in chaos now, with people standing and asking questions and expressing both shock and anger toward the stranger in their midst. The two security guards took a more forceful hold on Silas and moved him toward the door. Silas made eye contact with Smith. He saw nothing but the calm veneer that was painted over any vestige of emotion.

Then he was outside the library. The afternoon had grown cool; there was a wind blowing across the dusty field next to the building and grit got into Silas's eyes. "You guys going to take me for a long walk in the desert?" Silas rubbed his eyes.

The two men stood in front of the door, expressionless.

Silas tried to walk past them but one of the men put a hand on his chest. The man smiled. "Quit while you're ahead, Dr. Pearson. If we have to call Garfield County Sheriff's you'll be arrested for trespassing."

Silas looked past the men into the library. He could hear Senator Smith back at the podium, answering more awkward questions. Silas walked to his rental and drove away.

29

"I'M WORRIED ABOUT MY DAD," said Robbie.

"I'm worried about him too." Katie Rain sat across from Robbie in a well-appointed restaurant in Salt Lake's downtown. "Things have been pretty busy since I got back from Escalante. There are only three forensic anthropologists working for the FBI. I've had quite the backlog. But I'm glad we were able to get together."

"Like I said, I'm worried about him. He's . . . he's not taking this well."

"I think it's to be expected. My guess is that Silas is in shock. After five years of searching, hoping, preparing, now he's come face to face with the fact that his wife is dead."

They had ordered sandwiches and Robbie took a bite. "Is there anything you can do?" he asked after he'd taken a drink of water.

"No. I'm just part of the Evidence Recovery Team. Taylor is in charge. Like everything else, the FBI is very political, and Assistant Special Agent in Charge Taylor is in line to move up the ladder. The next Special Agent in Charge posting that opens up is likely to be his for the asking. He's not going to compromise that by letting a civilian—especially a foreign national—get in the way of an investigation."

"What about you? You seem to be walking a pretty fine line."

Katie shrugged. "I don't worry about these things too much. My job is to help the bureau solve crimes and to bring closure to grieving families. I guess I look at Silas and think, *Here's someone who needs closure.*"

"I think my dad likes you."

Katie laughed and then took a bite of her lunch. She finished chewing and said, "That sounds so high school." It was Robbie's turn to shrug. He blushed. Katie touched his hand. "I don't mean that in a condescending way. It's sweet. I like Silas too. He's kind and generous and I really feel for him."

"He told me that you went out and searched the Island in the Sky with him. You took a few days off work and everything."

"Yeah, it was last fall. A year ago. It's hard to believe; so much has happened since then. I sometimes wonder what it's like being inside your father's head. It must be a very busy place. A very frightening experience."

"I've always wondered what it was like to be inside his head too. He never let on much when we were kids, and then, well, and then he was gone."

"That couldn't have been easy."

"For me, it wasn't so hard. I was already older. I was twelve. But Jamie was just seven when Dad got the job at UNA. And then he met Penelope. They tried; every year they'd come up and we'd go down for a few weeks. We didn't make it easy on them, especially on Penelope. Jamie hated her; he blamed her for the end of my dad's marriage to my mom, even though Dad didn't meet Penny until after he'd taken the job in Flagstaff."

"It likely didn't matter. All a seven-year-old would see is the consequences. But you seem to be patching things up?"

"I am. The verdict is still out for Jamie. He's angry. Maybe always will be. I just want to get on with things; I want my father back, and if that means I have to make the moves, then I will. The Green River trip, even though it was morbid searching for a body every day, was pretty good, you know?"

"I know."

"Can I ask you something? It's about the case. If it means you're going to throw me in jail . . ."

She swatted him on the arm. "You can ask. I might not be able to answer."

"Dad has got it in for this Senator Smith, and I think with good reason. What I'm trying to figure out, however, isn't motive but means. It seems like there was a different MO in all three cases. To me, there doesn't seem to be any pattern between the three."

"The chloroform might be the pattern. Darcy's lungs were full of highly corrosive potash solution but we did find a trace of chloroform. With Penelope, however, there wasn't any lung tissue left to sample. So we don't know for sure. When our behavioral analysis unit did some work for us last spring they linked the McFarland and Pearce murders. They concluded that the intimacy of the crimes could be a connection between them. That and the fact that Pearce and McFarland knew one another."

"But Penelope looks like she was on her knees when she was shot. Isn't that right?"

"We think so, Robbie. Listen, I don't know if Silas would want to hear this."

"He knows. He's smart; he could see where the blood was, and where the bullet entered the rock. He figured it out. It means that she was either begging for her life, or executed, or both." There was a long silence between them. Robbie fiddled with his coffee cup. "Does the FBI have a new profile based on all of this?"

"We're looking to see if there is a connection. I don't think you have to work at Quantico to see that there is a strong relationship here. Pearce, McFarland, and your stepmother all knew one another;

all were killed in a way that suggests a personal connection between the killer and his or her victims. They were all killed close to the Colorado River. What we get is only a thumbnail, but what we believe is that all three victims knew their killer."

"And you think it's one killer, and not just three random murders?"

"We're proceeding as if they are all related, though not necessarily all the same killer. It's possible that all three killings are linked by motive, but different people carried out the murders."

"So who had motive?"

"That's out of my area of expertise."

"Dad told me you used to be a field agent."

"That was a long time ago."

"I bet you were good."

"I had some game."

"Let's pretend it's the old days then. Dad seems to be focused on this business of the resort in the Escalante because it was where Penelope died, and because she and her friends were fighting it in the years leading up to her death. Smith was supporting it, and Eleanor Barry, Jacob Isaiah, and Paul Love were all part of the team advancing the project. Dad's got a history with Isaiah and Love, as did Penelope. And Paul Love pulled a gun on Dad and his buddy Hayduke last spring. These guys all had millions of their own money on the line, and hundreds of millions in possible profits at stake. Maybe most damning of all was that Penelope and her friends were blackmailing the senator."

Rain stopped eating and raised an eyebrow.

"That's right. They had photos of him with Eleanor Barry; nothing too racy, but enough to stall, or maybe even sink, his career. They were lording them over Smith so that he would back down on his Colorado River Compact bill, which he did. They had given the photos to a reporter named Kresge with the *Tribune*, with the agreement that he would sit on them until the time was right, but he never got the chance to break the story."

"He died. In a car accident. I remember when that happened."

"Brakes went out on Soldier Summit."

"It's a nasty piece of highway between here and Price."

"Which is the senator's hometown."

"You think that Smith cut the lines?"

"Doesn't that sound familiar? Maybe it wasn't Smith himself. Maybe it was someone who works for him. The senator's assistant tried to kill Dad just last year doing the same thing on Comb Ridge. I think everybody thought that he just went crazy and tried to kill Dad, but maybe this is his thing. And there's something else. Have you heard the name Tabby Dingwall?"

"No, why?"

"His name was in the same file that Kresge had on Smith. Can you find out who he is?"

"You know, I got into forensic anthropology so I wouldn't have to run names through a database anymore." Rain was smiling when she said it. "I'll do it, but you have to do something for me. I need you to tell your father to back off Smith. And Eleanor Barry."

"I don't know—"

"Robbie, there's more going on than you both know. I can't get into it. But you've got to tell your father to back off."

"He won't listen to me. I tell him that he has to stop and it will—"

Rain's phone rang. She made an apologetic gesture and answered it. She listened and after a minute said, "I'm with him now." Robbie looked up. Then Rain said "okay," and hung up.

"Well, you might not have to have that conversation after all. Your dad just confronted a US senator at a town hall meeting and accused him of adultery and multiple homicides."

30

SILAS PEARSON STOOD NEXT TO his rental at a pull-out looking over the Escalante National Monument on the Hogsback road. The stone plateau was pocked with a hundred canyons capped with countless domes, reefs, and rises. Silas felt a wave of relief that he would no longer have to search this desolate and lonesome landscape.

He was startled when his cell phone buzzed in his pocket. He looked around as if he might find a cell tower but there was none. He looked at the call display and it read CALLER ID BLOCKED. He answered the ringing. "Pearson."

"It's Rain."

He breathed a sigh of relief. "It *is* raining out—over the V, where Harris Wash meets the Escalante River. You should see it."

"Silas, where are you?" He told her. "I just got a call from Agent Taylor."

"They sending you to bring me in?"

"No. But he's pretty pissed."

"And he thought that I would listen to *you* rather than him?"

"I'm calling as a friend. This is my personal cell. What you did back there in Boulder wasn't very smart. You have to stop. You've got to trust me that the FBI is going to do its job and catch whoever killed your wife. But you've got to stop acting like a bull in a china shop."

"Smith is guilty."

"Maybe. But that's not your job to determine. It's not even *our* job to determine that. Our job is to work with other law enforcement agencies to build a case and make an arrest. The District Attorney will then lay charges and a court will make a determination of guilt or innocence. You'll be involved in that, Silas, but what you are doing right now is going to destroy our case, if we even determine that Smith, Barry, or Isaiah are behind your wife's murder. I want you to cooperate with Taylor. Give him what information you have, and then leave it to his team to take it from there. I know that Penelope's murder is the most important thing in your world—"

"Of course it is! She was my wife!"

"I know, Silas, and I don't blame you for doing what you're doing, but you've got to trust me. If you don't step back, Taylor is going to arrest you."

"Is that what he told you to tell me?"

"He called me to see if I could reach out to you before it's too late."

"I think trusting you was a mistake." There was a long silence over the phone. Silas wondered if he had lost the cell signal on the wind.

"It wasn't a mistake, Silas. You can ask Robbie. We just spent two hours together. He's on his way back to Escalante now. But you've got to listen to me."

"I've got to go, Dr. Rain."

"Silas—"

He hung up. He threw the phone into the SUV and stood facing the wind for a long time.

"DON'T YOU START on me too." Silas sat in one of the hotel room's two chairs, a set of maps and books laid out over the table. Robbie was in the room's small kitchenette, microwaving dinner.

Robbie put the food down in front of his father. "I'm not starting on you. I'm just checking to make sure you know what you're doing."

"Five years, Robbie. And now we're getting close, and everybody wants me to back off. For most of my life I've just sat back and let things happen. That's the way it was with your mother, and that's the way it was with Penelope. *Easy come, easy go*, I always thought. I'm tired of being a pushover."

Robbie sat down and they started to eat. Silas drank beer from a can and played with his food. "I wanted to hit him. Standing up there, smug, that look on his face like he was invincible; I wanted to walk right up to him and punch him in the face."

"I think we'd be having this conversation through a Plexiglas wall if you did that."

"I know, but I don't care." Silas took a bite of his dinner and then pushed the plate away. "So, everything you've told me about Kresge and his car accident and the bribery, all of this was just sitting in some box of files in the archives of the *Tribune*? How is it that this didn't come out before?"

"Kresge was an old curmudgeon and didn't trust anybody else with the story. He sat on it. When he died, nobody went through his files. They just boxed it all up and put it in storage."

"What's this guy Harvey going to do with it?"

"He's starting to build the file from scratch, but without the source of the information, he's reluctant to do anything with it."

"And that source was Penny."

"And Kiel, and Darcy, it turns out."

"And this other guy whose name you say was on file, Tabby Dingwall?"

"That's right. Have you ever heard his name before? I'm going to go down to the Devil's Garden and look him up online."

"There is one other person who might know what's going on."

"Where is Mr. Hayduke?" asked Robbie.

"That's a good question. My guess is he's out in the Monument somewhere. If he was part of this band of friends working on taking down the Glen Canyon Dam, maybe he's got a copy of these photos, and can verify their validity."

"If he does, why hasn't he said anything about it so far?"

"That seems to be the way he is; it isn't until events start to crest that he shows up with some piece of missing information."

"And you don't think that's a little . . . strange?"

"I think it's a *lot* strange." Silas told Robbie about Hayduke's criminal record and history with PTSD. He filled his son in on Hayduke's recent hospital stay.

"I know this guy has been helpful over the last year—more than I have been—but I really don't like him. He's a few cans short of a six-pack, and that's saying a lot for a guy who thinks he's George Washington Hayduke."

"Maybe if you can find this Dingwall guy he'll know more about the photos. If he was friends with Penelope and the others, why hasn't he shown up before now? I need to find Hayduke and ask him about the photos. After that, I'll cut him loose. Sound alright?"

"Sounds like we have no choice."

31

THERE WAS A KNOCK AT the door to Silas's motel room. Robbie had been gone for an hour and he guessed that he had left without his key. When he opened the door, Katie Rain stood before him. "Buy a girl a drink?" she said, smiling.

"I'M SORRY," SILAS started after the pitcher of beer arrived. The restaurant was nearly empty. Robbie had been surprised to see them, but chose to continue on the computer terminal while Katie and Silas took a table and ordered beer.

"So am I. Taylor called and put some pressure on me and I agreed to call. I crossed the line between agent and friend. That's the way it's been since the start. He was taking advantage of that, and I shouldn't have let him. I'm sorry too."

"So you got in your car and drove for five hours just to tell me that?"

"I guess I did."

"So now what?"

"I don't know. We drink our beer. Let your kid do some cyber-sleuthing over there. Go for a hike in the desert under the moon?"

Silas smiled for the first time in what seemed like a month. "You're not going to tell me what's going on with Smith?"

"I can't. There's a line and I've crossed it but I can't do that."

Silas drank the rest of his glass of beer and refilled both of their mugs. He heard his son thanking the proprietor and then Robbie was next to him, his face drawn with concern.

"What is it, Rob?"

"Tabby Dingwall is—*was*—a Salt Lake City private investigator. He's been missing for the last six months."

THEY WERE BACK in their hotel room. Robbie picked up where he had left off. "Tabby Dingwall was a fifty-something ex-cop. I found a story on him in the *Tribune* from fifteen years ago. He was a detective with the Salt Lake City police. He shot a kid, a twelve-year-old. Kid was dressed up all gangster-style, had a plastic gun, was hanging out with some friends near a Shop N Go. Dingwall rolls up responding to a reported break-in nearby and the kid pulls the gun. The papers suggest the kid did it on a dare from his friends. Dingwall ordered the kid to drop the gun but he didn't. What happened next is conjecture, because Dingwall was riding alone and this was before Salt Lake City was carpeted in closed-circuit cameras. Dingwall in his hearing said the kid fired the gun and it made a sound like a twenty-two-caliber going off. The other kids who were there said they set off a firecracker. Whatever the case, Dingwall shot the kid, killing him.

"He was cleared of any wrongdoing, but he quit the force. His marriage went up in flames the following year. He didn't have any kids of his own, and here he was, in his mid-thirties and washed up. He started drinking. On a whim he signed up for a trip with the Southern Utah Wilderness Association. They went on a hike in Canyonlands. That was his turning point. I got all of this from the blog on his website. He got clean, got his PI license, and spent his downtime hiking in the canyons."

"Did he know Penelope?" asked Silas.

"He did."

"How do you know?"

Robbie reached into a folder and pulled out a sheet of paper. "This was on his blog. He called it Wilderness Investigations. Get it?" Robbie handed his father the sheet of paper. On it was a printed photograph.

Silas took it and in the yellow light of the kitchenette examined the image there. It was low quality, printed on a cheap printer on standard paper, but the faces staring back at him were clear enough.

"It's alright, Dad." Robbie put a hand on his father's knee.

"Silas, what is it?" Katie asked.

"It's a photograph of a group on a beach on the Colorado River. Kiel Pearce, Darcy McFarland, Tabby Dingwall, a clean-cut version of Josh Charleston, and Penny." Silas looked away and swallowed.

"They did a trip together in the spring seven years ago. I think that's how they all met." Robbie tapped the photo.

"Darcy and Penny had been friends before," Silas noted.

"But Josh and Tabby were on the trip. And Kiel was the guide." Robbie pointed to Pearce in the photo.

"Just like in the Monkey Wrench Gang," said Silas. "Do you remember in the spring when I was talking with Jane Vaughn's husband about her burial wishes?"

Katie nodded. "You went to Lee's Ferry."

"In her will it said that if Jane, Darcy, or Penelope died first, then the other two would take care of scattering their remains on the Colorado. It said 'the boys' were on their own. Dallas Vaughn and I thought that meant *us*. But it didn't. It meant Josh and Tabby."

Robbie nodded. "Dingwall went missing around the time that Kiel Pearce was killed. He had a client meeting set up and he never showed. He hasn't been seen since."

"You think it's possible that Dingwall is our guy? Was he involved in the business with the senator?" asked Silas.

"He could have been. He's either responsible somehow, or dead.

It seems pretty suspicious. Unstable ex-cop becomes wilderness-loving crusader. His friends start to go missing—get killed—and he takes a flyer just as the last of them gets knocked off."

"Not the last of them," said Silas. He was staring hard at the photo. He closed his eyes.

"When we were in Moab, right before the fire, I paid a visit to Jacob Isaiah's office."

"Silas, you didn't break in, did you?" asked Katie.

"Let's just say that it wasn't a social visit and leave it at that. One of the things I found was a set of personal files. He had one on Smith, on Barry, Love. He had one on Penny. There were photos in it: shots of her at a public event, shots of her having coffee. There were other files too, lots of names I didn't recognize. I think Tabby Dingwall was one of them."

Robbie said, "You think Dingwall was working for Isaiah—like a double agent—taking pictures, following Penny and the others?"

"I don't know. Maybe he was working for both Smith and Isaiah. I don't know. I need to get that file."

"No, you don't," said Rain. "You go back in there and anything that is in those files will be inadmissible in court. As it is, it's likely tampered evidence."

Silas tapped the arm of his chair, his head bobbing rhythmically up and down. "Maybe there's another explanation. Maybe Dingwall was straight-up with Penny. Maybe he was part of the gang. If that's the case, where is he?"

"I need to tell Taylor about this." Katie started to stand.

"And I need to find Josh. He's the only one left. He's likely in serious danger."

"The question is, danger from who?" asked Robbie.

"Everything points to Smith," said Silas.

"I'm not one hundred percent certain of that," Katie said, pulling a cell phone from her jeans. "I think Hayduke is in trouble, but I don't know that it's because of Smith. I'm going to call Taylor and tell him about this connection. I can't believe that the locals overlooked it."

"The FBI wasn't investigating Dingwall's disappearance?"

"No, it was Salt Lake County Sheriff's. We don't get involved unless the crime extends across state borders and I guess there was no reason to believe it had. This changes everything."

Rain stepped out of the motel room and onto the walkway that connected the second-storey rooms. Silas looked at his watch. It was almost ten at night. He found his cell phone and rummaged through his bag for his address book.

"You know you have an address book on your phone, don't you?"

Silas shot his son a look and found the number he was looking for. He dialed it. It was the number of the man Kiel Pearce had worked for. During Silas's investigation of that man's murder the previous spring they had spoken a few times. "Mr. Flint, it's Silas Pearson calling. I know it's late, I hope I didn't get you up or anything."

"Um, no, you didn't. I'm still at the office, actually. Sorry, you said it's Silas Pearson?"

"Yes, you might remember we talked last year, when one of your boatmen—"

"Shit, of course, Pearson. You were the one who found Kiel in Paria Canyon. Have you heard something about Kiel's murder? Have they found the killer?"

"Not yet, but I've got something I need to ask you. I've found— actually my son found—a photo of Kiel with a group that he led on the Colorado some years ago. All these people, except one, are now missing or dead."

"Holy shit."

"I was wondering if you could confirm for me when they did this trip together, who else was on the trip, and anything else you might think of that could be helpful."

"Sure, who's in the picture? I'll look them up in our customer files."

Silas told him the names.

"That's your wife, isn't it? I heard that a . . . that she had been found. I'm very sorry."

Silas could hear Flint tapping on some keys. "That was a private trip. Guy named Tabby Dingwall arranged it. He paid for it too. Just him, McFarland, your wife, and Charleston. I have a note here that they requested Kiel as the boatman. They did their own meals, so it was just the five of them."

"Dingwall paid?"

"That's right. There wasn't any problem with his check."

"How much?"

"It was four grand."

"I guess the PI business was good to him."

"I don't really have anything else here."

Silas thanked him and hung up. "Something tells me Tabby Dingwall was more than just a wilderness-loving PI."

32

KATIE RAIN WALKED BACK INTO the room and said, "Taylor is in Monticello and will assign an agent to do some digging. He is taking a connection between Dingwall's death and the others seriously."

"And what about Hayduke?" asked Silas.

"That's a good question. Where is he right now?"

"Last I saw him was the morning before I drove to Boulder. He said he was going to camp out in the Monument."

"Great, nearly two million acres of wilderness. He could be anywhere. We need to get him out of the desert and into a room where we can keep an eye on him and keep him safe until we figure out what happened to Tabby Dingwall. Taylor is going to call Kane and Garfield County, as well as the BLM, and ask them to keep an eye open for him."

"What about Smith?"

"Silas—"

"Katie, I know that you can't tell me the details. I just want to know where he is."

"He's left Utah."

"What? He was supposed to be on a tour of the area talking about the Compact."

"His office says there was urgent business in the Senate and he had to return to Washington on short notice. He canceled town halls in Hanksville and Green River."

"Urgent business, in the Senate? Give me a break."

"That's what his office says. Taylor says there are no votes scheduled. We know where he is, though."

"What are you talking about?"

"We know where he is. He's on a plane."

"How do you . . . you're watching him, aren't you? You've *been* watching him. For how long?"

"I can't say. But yes, we are keeping track of the senator."

Silas shook his head. "You know, if I hadn't gotten involved in this, there wouldn't be a case. You know that, right?"

"Silas, there is more to this than just Penelope's murder. You've got to trust me that this thing with Smith is more complex. I don't think Smith is your man, Silas. I don't think he killed Kiel or Darcy. I doubt he had someone else do it. Penelope was killed five years ago, and we aren't certain of Smith's day-to-day movements at that time, so it's *possible* he was involved in her death. Our theory, however, is that all three are related, so it stands to reason that he didn't kill her either. Tabby is a wildcard, so I can't even speculate on that."

"What aren't you telling me, Katie?"

"What I'm not telling you is that the FBI knows where Senator Smith was when Kiel and Darcy were killed. We know who he was talking to, and about what. Unless the man is Houdini, he isn't likely to have been involved in their deaths, at least not in a material way. If that's the case, then it stands to reason that he wasn't involved in Penelope's murder either."

"What about Kresge, the reporter?"

"I don't know anything about Kresge's death."

"Smith, or maybe someone who worked for him, could have been involved in that."

"It's a possibility, but that's not what the FBI is interested in. And don't ask, because I'm not going to tell you. I'm sorry, Silas, but if I cross that line, I'll be looking for a new job."

"You told me once that the FBI wouldn't fire you because you're one of three people doing your work for the G across the whole country."

"There are lines, and then there are *lines*. This is one of the lines you don't cross. Ever."

Silas rubbed his face. "So what about Hayduke?"

"Like I said, the local sheriff's offices and the BLM's law enforcement division have been notified. If they find him, they'll notify him of the situation and ask him to come in for a conversation."

"Of all the people in this photo, he's the only one we know is still alive."

"What else can we do?"

"I don't know what else the FBI can do, but in the morning, I'm going to go and look for him myself. He saved my life; I owe him that much."

AFTER KATIE HAD left, Robbie said, "I'm coming with you."

"I appreciate the offer, Rob, but I think we need to split up."

"Bad idea."

"Listen, Hayduke is *my* problem, not yours. I think it's pretty obvious that the two of you don't see eye to eye."

"He's crazy, Dad. I mean, yes, he's suffered a lot, and has PTSD, but he's also unbalanced in some other way. This whole Hayduke act is some kind of manic response to the commotion that's raging in his head all the time. You can see it in his eyes. I think he's genuinely nuts."

"He's a vet. He probably saw a lot while he was in Iraq."

"Did he? Do you know for sure that he was overseas?"

"I take his word for it. And Taylor told me he was recently in a hospital recovering from some PTSD-related issues after the shooting on the Arizona Strip in the spring."

"I'm going to check him out."

"Good. Do it. And while you're at it, I wonder if you can try to find out what the hell Katie was talking about with regards to Senator Smith."

"If the FBI is conducting some other investigation, it's not like it's going to be on the internet."

"No, but maybe you could look further into the relationship between Barry, Isaiah, Love, and Smith and see if there's anything there."

"Like campaign contributions?"

"Sure, start there. I wonder if there's more to it than that. What else does the FBI investigate other than murder?"

"A lot. Terrorism, to start with."

"They thought Penelope was a terrorist."

"What? That's ridiculous."

"A domestic terrorist. They thought that she wanted to blow up Glen Canyon Dam."

"Your Penelope? That wasn't her style."

"No, it wasn't, but the FBI had a file on her. On Darcy McFarland too. And on Hayduke."

"Now *him* I could see. That's what Hayduke wanted to do in *The Monkey Wrench Gang*, wasn't it? Blow up the dam?"

"Yeah, but it never happened. They couldn't even blow up a couple of bridges. None of that stopped the feds from snooping on Penelope. Smith doesn't seem like the terrorist sort, unless you count his campaign to destroy Utah's wilderness. If Penelope was here she'd tell you it constituted a kind of terrorism."

"What about white-collar crime? You know, embezzlement?"

"Maybe . . ."

"You know what the top priority among criminal investigations is, according to the FBI website? Public corruption: dirty politicians on the take, defrauding the American people."

"Can you find out?"

"I don't know, Dad. You heard Katie. It's a line she can't cross."

"I don't think Katie can be any help. What about your reporter friend in Salt Lake? Maybe this is connected to Kresge's death?"

"I can try. I can also see if there is a non-profit organization in Washington that investigates this sort of thing. I know there is in Canada, so there must be one in the States. Do you really think this will help find who killed Penelope?"

"I don't know. I think this all relates back to Penelope blackmailing Smith. That's how this started, or at least it seems like it. Maybe Smith killed Penelope to stop her from doing anything with the photos of him and Barry. And then, when he found out Kresge had copies too, he arranged for him to have an 'accident.' Just like I almost had an accident on Comb Ridge last year. You know, now that I think about it, I wonder if Smith *was* behind *that* too?"

"They arrested someone for that, Dad. I think you're getting ahead of yourself."

"If Smith killed Penelope because she had these photos, who killed the others? If Penny was blackmailing Smith to get him to drop his proposed changes to the Colorado River Compact, wouldn't he have had to kill everyone involved? Katie said Smith was already under surveillance when McFarland and Pearce died. Dingwall went missing about the same time as Pearce was killed."

"Dingwall is the missing piece right now, isn't he?" Silas asked. "Nobody knows where he is. Maybe he isn't dead. Maybe he's involved."

"Dad, it stands to reason that Dingwall took the pictures of Smith and Barry. How *could* he be involved?"

"I don't know. None of this makes any sense."

"Let's get some sleep. In the morning, I'll dig into this. You can go and warn Hayduke that he's the last man standing. We'll meet back here at the end of the day and compare notes. Alright?"

Silas nodded. There was no way for him to know that they wouldn't be meeting at the end of the day to compare anything, especially notes.

33

SILAS PLANNED TO SYSTEMATICALLY SEARCH each of the side roads that led off the Hole in the Rock Road until he found Hayduke's Jeep. The Harris Wash road was rough, but beyond the Wash itself the road became even rougher. A sign at Harris Wash warned travelers from proceeding any farther without four-wheel drive. The brand-new Ford Explorer he had rented seemed capable, but when he reached a place where the trail descended precariously on an off-set angle, Silas stopped. If Hayduke was on the steep, sandy road toward the V where Harris Wash met the Escalante, he was on his own.

He decided to go back to the main road and drive to Egypt, another jumping-off point for hikes into the Escalante. Several times he bottomed the Explorer out, hearing the skid plate crack on high-center rocks or drag along a deep rut in the road. Silas winced and tried to remember if his insurance covered this sort of damage.

At Egypt trailhead, with the convoluted earth of the Escalante Basin before him, he looked among the dozen vehicles parked there for the gunmetal Jeep. It wasn't there. There was a breeze blowing from the west, and Silas could see, for the third day in a row, thunderheads amassing on the horizon. The wind smelled faintly of rain.

He drove two more spur trails before searching the campground at Devil's Garden. The place was empty but tire tracks in the sand and signs of a campfire suggested someone had been there the night before. Silas drove toward Dance Hall Rock.

It was late in the afternoon when he reached the dome of sandstone that jutted from the slickrock plateau. He stopped short of it and switched off the engine. The temperature had dropped quickly and the wind was blowing dust into his eyes. There was nobody around.

Silas took a few tentative steps forward. The wind pushed him back. In the late afternoon light the earth that surrounded Silas seemed drawn, the shadows long, the clefts in the stone filled with gloom. He managed another hundred yards and stopped in the lee of the monolithic stone.

"Hayduke?" he called. Something made him shout a second time, "Hayduke!"

There was no response. "Penelope?" he said, more softly, the word swallowed by the wind.

There was no answer. He stood, unable to approach the place where his wife had met her end. Unable to face the spot where someone had ordered, or forced, her down on her knees and shot her between the eyes. Someone had executed her for something she knew, had done, or might do in the future.

She was not there. And now, Silas knew, she was nowhere.

HE DROVE BACK through the darkness, the last light clinging to the Kaiparowits Plateau. He was about to pass the turn-off to Devil's Garden without a second thought, but through the gargoyles of sandstone that haunted the place he saw the lick of a windblown fire in the campground. He jammed the wheel of the Explorer and took the road down into the draw.

A fire burned in a metal grill. The Jeep was parked nearby.

Silas pulled into a nearby campsite and shut the motor down on the Explorer. He couldn't see Hayduke. He could smell rain in the air.

Silas walked to where the fire cracked and spit sparks into the opaque sky. There was a camp chair set up. A few empty cans of beer lay scattered on the ground, but there was no other sign of Hayduke. Silas went to check the Jeep. No Hayduke. Silas poked his head inside. Duffle bags, a rope, a rack of climbing gear, a backpack, half a dozen surplus ammo cans, and a flat of beer littered the back. A hunting rifle and a carbine were tucked among the luggage and gear.

Silas considered the collection of ammo cans. The green boxes were surplus from the Vietnam War; they had been used to store and transport belts of ammunition for large-caliber machine guns. The ammo cans had been manufactured in the millions, and after the war they had become a favorite accessory for river-runners: they could easily be secured to the frame of a raft and were virtually waterproof.

Silas looked in the front of the Jeep: more beer cans on the floor, a few topo maps, a Utah state road map, and a few books. Tucked between the front seats was the first edition copy of *Desert Solitaire* that he had given Hayduke the previous fall after the incident on Comb Ridge. He picked it up, flipped the book open, and reread the inscription. The young man obviously appreciated the gift. Silas was about to return it when he saw something that made his heart catch in his throat.

The spine of Penelope's journal was protruding from next to the driver's side seat, wedged between it and the hand brake. Silas reached for it and pulled it out. He felt perspiration trickling down his back and forming under his arms.

"Hey, what the fuck . . . ? Oh, shit, it's you."

Silas slipped the journal inside his coat and grabbed the Abbey book. He turned quickly to watch Hayduke holster his .357; his face broke into a wolfish grin. Silas turned with the book in his hand. "I see you still have this?"

"Yeah, of course. It's pretty much the most important thing to me in the world. So, what are *you* doing out here, and why are you fucking with my shit?"

34

"YOU'RE IN TROUBLE, JOSH. I came to warn you. I've been driving all over the Hole in the Rock Road today looking for you."

"I was up on the Straight Cliffs, looking around for places where my namesake and ol' Seldom Seen might have hung out. What kind of trouble am I in?"

"You want a beer?" Silas went to his SUV and grabbed a six-pack and the photo Robbie had printed off Tabby Dingwall's blog. He handed Hayduke a beer and opened one for himself. He drank and then handed Hayduke the photo.

"Do you know Tabby Dingwall?"

Hayduke studied the photo. Through his beard Silas couldn't tell if the young man was smiling. The light from the fire played with the deep shadows on his face. He held the photo and looked at it as he guided the beer can to his mouth. Silas thought the young man's eyes looked red, though that too might have been from the firelight. "Do you know him, Hayduke?"

"Yeah, I know him. What kind of trouble am I in?"

"Tabby Dingwall is missing. He's been missing for six months. Everybody in that photo is either dead or missing—"

"Or sitting right here with you."

"Hayduke, you're in danger. Whoever killed Penelope, whoever killed Kiel and Darcy and whoever, well, made this Tabby Dingwall guy disappear, will likely come for you next."

Hayduke, unconcerned, took another long pull on the can of beer. He continued to study the photo. "This was a good trip," he said. "This was a long time ago, man. Look at me! A clean-cut kid! I was just back from Iraq, what, maybe a year then? Just out of the service. I thought I'd do some wilderness stuff, like around here, climb some of the peaks, do a river trip or two. *This* was a great trip. I had met Pen and the others and they invited me along on this gig they had going. A private trip sort of thing. I mean, what a blast! Just the five of us on the river for three weeks. It was pretty awesome. I mean, the food was pretty basic because we didn't have a cook, but the solitude! We saw a few other groups while we were on the river, but because we were a small outfit we could camp at some of the more secluded beaches. It was incredible."

"So you knew *all* of them."

"Of course," Hayduke waved the picture around. He finished his beer and tossed the can into the pile next to him.

"Shit, man, we had big plans. We were going to change things around here. We were going to make a difference. Penelope had the plan, of course. She was the one who thought things through. She knew what we had to do to get it done; she knew how to do it. She was definitely in charge."

"What was Tabby's role?"

"Shit, he was one burned-out motherfucker. He was cooked. He killed a kid; did you know that? Fuck, even with my two years in Iraq, *I* never killed a kid. Lots of rag-heads and probably more than one or two women, but never a kid. Not that I know of at least. Lots of bullets flying around, mind you, so who the fuck really knows, right? But Tabby—he popped a kid in front of a fucking Shop N Go. He never got over it. Spent years with the barrel of his fucking

154

piece in his mouth every goddamned night. Then he met Penelope at a SUWA meeting—"

"SUWA?"

"Southern Utah Wilderness Association. She took Tabby for a hike in the Grand Gulch, showed him the cliff dwellings, the kivas, all that shit, and Tabby stopped thinking about offing himself every minute of the day."

"Did you get along with him?"

"Tabby? Sure. We were like brothers."

"When did you see him last?"

"Oh man, it's been a long time. You see, when Penny disappeared, we all just stopped hanging out, doing shit together. She was the glue. We came . . . unstuck after she disappeared. Kiel, he was always the least committed, so he went back to guiding full time. Darcy stayed in Flag and did her thing there. Tabby took the whole thing pretty hard. Me and him, we even tried to find Pen for awhile. You know, looked around, kind of like you did, but without the dreams and the maps all over the walls. But he had bills to pay, so he kept on doing his Dick Tracy thing up in Salt Lake. And me, well, I just carried on, you know what I mean?"

The fire popped and Hayduke reached behind himself and put a few more pieces of juniper on the flames. "You got another beer?" he asked. Silas handed him one and opened a second for himself.

"Why didn't you tell me all this last year when we met?"

"I wanted to, but I thought that you wouldn't want my help if I told you about everybody. And then shit started to go down, you know what I mean? First Darcy, and then Kiel. I didn't want to spook you."

"You wouldn't have spooked me; we could have worked together. We might have even kept Tabby from going missing."

"Tabby was a big boy; he could look after himself. I doubt very much there was anything that you, or me, could have done for him."

"Do you know what happened to him?"

"I got my suspicions. Isn't that what you're here to tell me about?"

"I guess it is. But it's a bloody mess and I don't really understand much of it myself anymore."

"Try it out on me, and let's see where it gets us."

Silas told him about his confrontation with the senator, and Katie Rain's admission that Smith was under investigation, but not for Penelope's murder. He told him about what he found in Isaiah's office.

"I don't believe it for one fucking second," Hayduke said, tossing another beer can on the ground. "From where I stand it all lines up. Isaiah, Love, Barry, Smith: they're all in on this."

"That's what I wanted to ask you about. It was Tabby that got the pictures of Barry and the senator."

"Yeah, he was doing her when he was mayor of Salt Lake, and we figured that it was likely still going on. Tabby got the pictures himself, you see? Pen didn't want any part of it. She wanted a fair fight, but Tabby was a street cop, a scrapper. He wanted to put some insurance in the bank, so he followed Smith when he was in Salt Lake, and sure enough, Barry shows up. He didn't get any porn shots, just the two of them holding hands, kissing, but it was enough. Tabby and the rest of us talked it through. It was a bit of a row, actually. In the end we decided to use it as insurance."

"Against what? The Colorado River Compact?"

"That's what this is all about, Silas. Everything. You must know that. All these places, all these landscapes, it still all comes down to the Colorado River. It's the heart of the desert, of the canyon country. It's the big enchilada. It's all Penelope cared about. I can't fucking believe you didn't see that."

Silas fiddled with the tab on his beer can. "It would have been a lot easier if you had just spelled it out for me from the start."

"I'm sorry," Hayduke said. "I've got a big fucking mouth. But what I'm trying to say is, yes, it's about the Compact. If Smith had gotten his way—if he *gets* his way—then the feds would have had the power to refill Lake Powell without having to coddle the lower basin states. Shit, the water level is down to less than fifty percent. If Smith passes his bill, then Utah can tell the lower basin states to go fuck themselves, and hide behind the Bureau of Reclamation to do it. They could shut the tap on Glen Canyon Dam and just let a trickle through for the next ten years. I mean, we're still talking about a huge amount of water—something like seven or eight million acre-feet a year—but it would violate the Law of the River, not to mention our treaty with Mexico.

"That water is big money. Power for a million-plus people. Beaucoup dollars coming from that. Last I heard more than a hundred and twenty-five mill each year. And the recreation dollars! You know how much Paul Love could rent a slip on that new marina for? Our old pals Jacob Isaiah and that Barry woman stand to make a mint if they can build their Escalante Resort.

"They say to hell with the Grand Canyon; to hell with all the endangered fish downstream. Fuck the Mexicans. Smith's bill would have given the feds the power to turn off the spillway and destroy Glen Canyon for a second time. It would have killed us. It would have killed Pen. So we did what we had to do."

"You blackmailed a US senator."

"We did what we thought was necessary. It wasn't like we set out to do it. It was our only chance to kill Smith's bill."

"How did the reporter, Kresge, get involved?"

"He was our insurance policy. Pen knew him. He covered politics. She gave him a package of information, but embargoed it. She told him that he could only use the images if she said so."

"How did that work? These days if a reporter had a scandalous story like the Smith-Barry affair, they would run with it, consequences be damned."

"Tabby had something on Kresge too."

"Really? What?"

"Sleeping with a source. Not Penelope; no way. But Kresge was a sleazeball too. Everybody has something they don't want to go public, so Tabby got something on Kresge, and that way we could control the story."

"So you told Smith what you had on him?"

"That was Penelope's job. I said I'd do it, but by then I was looking less like a clean-cut vet and more like, well, more like—"

"More like Hayduke."

"Yeah, so Penny volunteered. She met with Smith in the spring five years ago. We had it all lined up. Smith was going to introduce the Bill the next week. He had the votes, but just barely. It was going to be tight. So Pen met with him and laid it out. I guess they got at it pretty good. Smith had her tossed from his office down in Blanding. But he thought about the consequences. The man wants to be president; did you know that? He's got an exploratory committee and everything. I don't know how he thinks fucking over California will help him, given that they have fifty-five electoral college votes, but I guess he figures a wild-eyed Mormon conservative from Utah will never win California anyway. So he thinks it over and decides to kill his bill. Says that it would be too expensive, cost the country too much during a time of austerity. The country was hurting, so it made sense."

"But you think he didn't leave it alone?"

"No way he left it alone. He killed Penelope, and he killed Kresge."

"Penny told him who had the story?"

"Fuck no, he must have figured that out on his own. It wouldn't take much. There's only so many national political reporters in Utah. He must have narrowed it down."

"But there wasn't any investigation into Kresge's death?"

"Smith made it look like an accident. Just like you on Comb Ridge. Just a brake malfunction on one of the most dangerous roads in Utah. Who's going to investigate a US senator for murder? It was a perfect crime."

"How did Smith know that with Kresge dead the photos wouldn't simply fall into the hands of the next reporter down the food chain?"

Hayduke seemed to stare into the flames for a long time, his face a mask of contemplation.

"How did he know?"

"I don't know. I have no idea. Maybe he had some pull at the paper? I don't know."

"It seems like one hell of a risk to take for a man who wants to be president. I mean, there's been more than one sex scandal on the road to the White House, but murder? That's tough to get over."

"Don't fucking kid yourself, Silas. You Canadians think politics isn't a blood sport, but it is. Lots of presidents have had lots of people killed for political gain. Look at that motherfucker Bush. He sent more than four thousand Americans and more than a hundred thousand Iraqis to the grave, and all so he could win a second fucking term and continue to give blowjobs to the oil and gas companies."

Silas felt his cell phone buzz in his pocket: an incoming text message. There was practically no cell reception anywhere in the Monument, but he had found that from time to time, depending on the wind direction and cloud cover, he could occasionally send and receive texts. He ignored it for the time being. "That's a little different than cutting someone's brake lines or shooting someone in cold blood."

"Yeah, with the Iraq thing we committed war crimes against a whole nation; with Pen and Kresge and the others it was simple ideological differences."

"Are you saying that Smith killed, or had *all* these people killed, just because they disagreed with him?"

"Sure, it happens all the time."

"It doesn't happen all the time. You don't kill people just because they have a different point of view."

"You kill them because their point of view threatens yours; because their point of view is getting in the way of what you want."

"I thought you said Smith had them killed because of the blackmail."

"Yeah, I guess so."

Silas watched him through the fire.

"You didn't agree with that strategy, did you?"

"Penny didn't, but Darcy and Tabby thought it was the only way to stop the Compact Bill. Kiel just went along with whatever they said. Pen didn't like it, but she agreed it was the only way."

"What about you?"

"The Compact didn't matter one fucking way or another, man. It was just another piece of paper, just another bunch of people *talking*, rather than *doing* something. I am sick to death of listening to people talk about all this shit. Saving the desert, saving the canyons. Free the Colorado! And then, at the end of the goddamned day, what we get is a sludge-filled sewage lagoon where there was once a wild and beautiful river. People think that because you can wade through houseboaters' shit to Cathedral in the Desert again that everything is alright, and we should be happy with what we have. It's bullshit! The goal is to destroy that motherfucking dam. To smash it to pieces, to see the Colorado running free once more. C. Thorn Smith's bill would have drowned the Glen a second time; we wouldn't let that happen, but someone figured that stopping Smith from filling up the reservoir again was good enough. It was a total fucking betrayal."

"Who betrayed who? What are you talking about?"

"Nothing, man, I'm not talking about nothing. The goal was never to just stop Smith, that's all I'm saying. Give me another beer, would you?"

Silas threw Hayduke a beer and opened the last one on the ring for himself. He watched the young man drink half of the can in one long pull. "What are you going to do now? You're the last person from that photograph alive."

"You don't know that. Tabby could be out there. Maybe he got spooked. Maybe he's hiding out." Hayduke looked down at the sheet of paper in his hand. In his anger he'd partially crumpled it up. He smoothed it out on his leg and while finishing the can of beer he looked at it. He leaned forward and laid it down on the coals of the fire. It instantly ignited and burned, sending the tattered residue to rise up on convection currents of heat into the night sky.

Silas watched him. Hayduke remained immobile, staring at where the photo had been in the flames. Silas considered the young man's predicament: he was the last man standing of the five friends who had stared down a US senator, blackmailing him, and risking their lives in doing so. It had cost them, and now this young man was all that stood in the way of someone getting away with murder and reintroducing a bill in the Senate that would drown Glen Canyon yet again.

Then Silas thought again: Hayduke was the last man standing.

35

"I GOT TO TAKE A piss." Hayduke rose heavily from his chair and walked off into the darkness. Silas watched the fire and then regarded the dark, heavy sky above. It would almost certainly rain before the night was out. He waited a long time before Hayduke returned, another six-pack in his hairy hand. Something about how Hayduke walked triggered a memory. He seemed to be favoring his injured leg. He offered Silas one. Both men opened the beer. "Sorry, it's a little warm. No ice."

Silas continued to regard him. He'd listened to his speech but despite the young man's bluster, Silas had something else on his mind. "So, you still have that copy of *Desert Solitaire*?"

"Of course! It's my most treasured possession."

"Penelope got that signed by Abbey. Did you know that?"

"I knew he had signed it."

"Yeah, when she was an undergrad. She found the first edition copy in a bookstore in Tucson and when he was doing a signing there, after he released *The Fool's Progress*, she got him to sign *Solitaire* too. She said they talked for almost ten minutes. The rest of the lineup was getting pretty agitated, and the bookstore owner made her step aside. He asked her to have a drink with him afterwards, but she declined."

"Why?"

"Because he had a reputation."

"So what, man? Have the drink; what could it hurt?"

"She didn't. And he died a year later."

"That's the way she was, you know. Always morally superior."

"What are you talking about?"

"Penny. That's the way it was with her sometimes. She was quick to take the high road, to point out when you were on the low road."

"How is that a bad thing?"

"It's not, I guess. It was really fucking annoying sometimes. That's the way it was with the Glen, you know what I mean?"

"I have no idea what you're talking about."

"It's nothing, man. Forget about it."

Silas felt a raindrop on his head. He looked up at the sky and another one hit his cheek. "I, ah, I noticed, Hayduke, that you had Penelope's notebook in your Jeep."

There was a long silence. A few more drops of rain hit the fire, making a hiss. Hayduke sat still, facing the flames, the can of warm beer in his left hand.

"Did you break into my house and steal it?"

Again, a long silence.

"Hayduke—"

"I fucking heard you!" he exploded. "I heard you the first fucking time."

"You did, didn't you?"

"Yeah, I broke in and stole it. I needed it. There are places in that journal that still need to be saved, man. I needed to know what Penelope had in mind for her Ed Abbey National Monument plan. I needed the journal."

"Why didn't you just ask?"

"I don't know." Hayduke was quiet again.

"I would have let you see it."

"I said I don't know!"

"So you drove down to my place in the Castle Valley that night, the night when my bookstore burned down, and broke into my house? I thought you were up in the La Sals that night."

"I was. It's a short drive. Only like an hour."

"Were you in Moab?"

Hayduke looked at him. The flames had burned up around another piece of juniper and there was a red glow in the man's eyes.

"Did you come through Moab? You knew I wasn't going to be home, didn't you. You knew that I wasn't in the Castle Valley. You knew exactly where I was."

"I don't know what you're talking about, man. I went to your place to ask you for the journal and when you weren't there, I just . . . let myself in. You told me you kept the journal hidden and there were only so many places."

"You broke into my place."

"I just . . . yeah, fuck, I broke in. Shit, it wasn't hard. I didn't even have to wreck anything. I just popped the lock. You really should get a better set-up. When I was in Iraq we used to slip in and out of places all the time, no big deal."

"This isn't Iraq. Why didn't you just come to the store? You must have known where I was."

Hayduke was silent. He drank his beer.

"You *did* know where I was. You *were* in Moab." Silas closed his eyes. In the time it took for the fire to pop and send sparks into the sky, two images aligned in his mind. One of them was Hayduke limping as he walked back from the Jeep just now, warm beer in his hand. The second image was that of a man with a Molotov cocktail in his hand, moving awkwardly but confidently before tossing the bomb into Silas's bookstore. Silas had convinced himself that the limp was that of an old man—Jacob Isaiah—but it wasn't. It was the limp of a young man who had recently been injured. "You were at the store. It was you I saw through the window. It was you."

36

"YOU BETTER STOP NOW, DR. Pearson. Just stop now." Hayduke hadn't moved. He sat still in his camp chair, his left hand pressing into the flimsy tin of the beer can.

"Did you burn my store down?"

Hayduke shifted his weight now. He finished the beer and tossed the can into the flames. The paint on it began to bubble almost immediately. He pushed himself to standing.

"You got to take a leak again?"

"Fucking Mormon beer is like water."

"You're not going to answer my questions?"

"I think you've gone off the deep end, dude. I think you've finally lost your marbles. Those dreams you've been having? You're having a psychotic break."

"So that's a no? I need to hear you say it."

"I went to your place to ask you for the journal, but you weren't there. Yeah, I broke in. I'm sorry, okay? It was my goddamned journal too. It was all of ours! Penelope just happened to keep it. That's all. It was mine too."

"It was a personal journal. It was Penelope's deepest thoughts on wilderness, on the west, on her love of these places."

"I got to take a piss." Hayduke walked off in the opposite direction from the last time, into the darkness beyond his Jeep and then past Silas's rented Explorer. Silas watched him disappear into the darkness. It was raining harder now. He felt his short, spiky hair growing damp. He wanted to rise and get a hat from the Explorer, but he couldn't stand. His legs felt as if they had been set in concrete. His phone buzzed again to remind him that he had an unread text. He fished it from his pocket and flipped it open, rainwater gathering on the LCD display.

He read the text and then read it again. Everything he thought he knew about the world for the past five years collapsed around him.

THE GUNSHOT WAS so loud that Silas jumped, knocking over his beer and almost dropping his phone in the fire. The sound echoed off the Straight Cliffs. The second shot made him stand up. The roar of the discharge was very close. Along with the second shot Silas heard an explosion of air. Then there was a third and fourth shot in rapid succession. Silas stood, peering into the darkness, the sound of the gunfire still reverberating in his ears.

Hayduke walked past his Jeep and into the circle of light by the fire. He held his .357 Magnum revolver in his hand. "Well, Dr. Pearson," he said, "It looks as if you've gone and fucked up another car. Hope you took the insurance on that rental, because they are going to be pissed at you."

"What have you done?"

"I shot the shit out of your Ford."

Silas took a step toward Hayduke. "What have you done?"

Hayduke raised the revolver and pointed it at Silas. "It's not what I've done that you should be worried about. It's what I'm about to do. Sit the fuck down."

Silas didn't move.

"I have two rounds left in the cylinder. Either one of them would take a limb off from this distance. Now: Sit. The fuck. Down."

Silas stepped back and sat on the edge of his camp chair.

"Give me your phone." Silas hesitated. Hayduke thumbed the hammer of the heavy pistol. "I swear to God I'll blow your brains all over this campsite. Give me your phone, *now*." Silas took the phone out. "Just toss it, underhand."

Silas did as he was told. Hayduke caught the phone with his left hand. He flipped it open and the LCD display shone brightly in the dark night. Hayduke grinned his wolfish smile. "How sweet. Your girlfriend Katie Rain sending you a warning. I wondered how long before the FBI connected the dots. I guess I didn't see them making *that* connection though."

"Josh, why?"

"It's still fucking Hayduke to you, Dr. Pearson. And we're not getting into any of that right now." Hayduke closed the phone and tossed it into the fire. "What we are going to do is play a little game. That's right; don't look at me like that. We're going to play a game called 'Hayduke Lives.'"

"Josh, I'm not going to play any game with you—"

"You'll play it or I kill you right now."

Hayduke Lives. Figures, thought Silas: Edward Abbey's final book, one most critics thought he hadn't actually finished before he died.

"Here's how the game works. I'm going to drive away right now, and you, well, you're going to have to figure out what to do next. All on your own this time. No Hayduke to lead you to the next clue. No Hayduke to lead you from one dot to the next. But here's the thing, Dr. Pearson. We're not the only players in this game, so you had better figure things out quickly."

"What are you going to do?"

"If I told you, I'd spoil the end of the story, wouldn't I?" Hayduke started to back away. The light from the fire caused the long, silver barrel of the revolver to glow red. He reached the Jeep and opened the driver-side door. "If you get up I'm going to shoot your leg off and let you bleed to death out here."

Hayduke sat down in the Jeep; its engine roared to life. Silas lunged toward the vehicle, but Hayduke was already gunning the engine, its thick tires spinning in the wet mud. He grabbed the vehicle's canvas roof, tearing at it for a handhold, but Hayduke was accelerating and Silas was thrown from the vehicle onto the road. He lay there in the muck and watched the Jeep race up the track and disappear over the rise. He heard it once more after a few seconds, and then he was alone in the darkness, the rain falling heavily now, the storm pressing down on the circling desert.

37

KATIE RAIN SAT IN HER motel room. It was early in the morning, and Silas Pearson had just left to search the desert for the misanthropic Josh Charleston, AKA Hayduke. She had watched him drive off in the rented Explorer and then called Dwight Taylor.

"What have you got?"

"Not much. Silas has gone off to look for Charleston. He's still pretty much convinced that Smith is behind all of this. The photo that his son pulled off of Tabby Dingwall's website showing McFarland, Pearce, de Silva, Dingwall, and Charleston all together has him more convinced than ever that Smith is responsible for each of their deaths, and that Charleston is the last man standing."

"That's one interpretation."

"Well, he's gone looking."

"That's a needle in a haystack operation."

"He knows him pretty well. He figures he's out in the Escalante somewhere."

"Big somewhere."

"What's going on with Smith?"

"We're taking him today."

"Where?"

"He's flying back to Salt Lake this afternoon. He probably figures he's dodged the bullet, leaving town for DC and now coming back. Misdirection. We'll take him at the airport."

"You going to be there?"

"No, the Salt Lake field team will make the arrest. My job is done, for now."

"What about Barry and Isaiah?"

"That's my reward for the last two years. We'll nab Barry while Smith is on the plane. I get to go and have a visit with Jacob Isaiah in person at the same time. Agent Nielsen is in Escalante now. You guys should hook up for coffee. Bring your vest and your piece."

"We'll see. I'm on vacation right now, remember?"

"You know that the Special Agent in Charge doesn't like this one bit. You're much too close to Pearson."

"That's the way it goes, Dwight. If he wants to fire my ass, he can go ahead. Sometimes I think I'd rather be teaching, working eight months of the year and lying on a beach in Togo the rest of the time."

"Bodies getting to you, Rain?"

"No, it's all these living, breathing people that are getting to me. Smith's flagrant misappropriation of funds and its contrast to a good, honest investigation like that of the de Silva case makes me wonder what I'm doing."

"Don't talk like that. The Smith thing is a solid bit of police work. This guy has siphoned nearly twenty million dollars of public money from the American Recovery and Reinvestment Act into the pockets of people like Eleanor Barry and Jacob Isaiah. In return they've made a million dollars in donations to Smith's Political Action Committee. He's going to run for president using money that he stole from the American people."

"I'm not saying it isn't a good case. I'm just saying I wish I never had to think about it. I'd rather be finding whoever killed Penelope de Silva."

"Me too. We're getting there. The lab called and told me they will have ballistics to me later today. If I get anything interesting, I'll call. Thanks for doing what you can on this, Katie."

"I'm doing it to protect Silas. That's why I'm here."

"I'll take what I can get."

"MY DAD LEFT early. He's out driving around the Monument looking for Hayduke . . . for Josh Charleston. I'm getting pretty sick and tired of calling him that ridiculous name."

"What are *you* going to do?"

"Grab some breakfast. Then I'm going to plug in and see what else I can find out about what Josh has been doing these last few months."

"He's been in the hospital, hasn't he?"

"Sure. But not the whole time. He disappears for days and weeks at a time. He says he's camping. Hiking. I don't know. I think he's scheming."

"What's he scheming?"

"That's what I want to find out."

"KATIE, IT'S DWIGHT. Where are you?"

"I'm in my hotel room. Are you still at work? I thought the Smith thing was over hours ago. By the way, you looked good standing behind the Special Agent in Charge during the interview. What is he, five foot six? You looked like the not-so-friendly giant."

"The Smith operation is over for now, but Quantico is open twenty-four hours. I just got a call about ballistics. I leaned on them this afternoon; I was getting antsy. We've got a major problem. Remember last year we dug slugs out of the rock along the highway over Comb Ridge? The slug we dug out of the stone at Dance Hall Rock matches the ones we dug out of the stone at Comb Ridge."

"Charles Nephi, Smith's former aide!"

"No, not *his* slugs. Josh Charleston's!"

"Holy shit."

"There's more. I'm not happy about this. Remember when Silas's store went up in flames? We had two cameras from traffic intersections in Moab that we needed to check. It got put on the back burner but I called about it today. Josh Charleston's Jeep was on one of those cams, going into and out of Moab that evening. I've got Eugene on it. He's got a small team in Escalante, and is mobilizing Garfield County Sheriff's deputies. Have you heard from Silas? He was out looking for Charleston."

"He's out in the Monument right now. I haven't heard from him all day. I'll try calling and texting him as soon as we get off the phone."

"I hope for his sake he hasn't found him."

38

ROBBIE PEARSON LEFT THE PIZZA parlor on Main Street at nine. It was dark out and the rain was falling hard on the pavement. It was cooler and the world smelled fresh. Despite this, Robbie wore a look of deep concentration. He had spent most of the day on his cell phone and using the internet. It had only been in the last few hours that he had learned what Hayduke *had* been doing for the last few months.

Robbie was surprised to see that his father's rental wasn't parked outside of the hotel. He walked to the second-storey landing and unlocked the door. The room was hot and stuffy but empty. He put down the stack of printouts on the table in the kitchenette, washed his hands, and got a can of beer from the fridge. He was taking a deep drink when there was a knock at the door. He put the beer can down on the counter and walked across the room. He looked through the peephole and then opened the door a crack.

"Hey, shit, is it ever fucking raining!"

Robbie hesitated.

"Good Christ, I'm wet. You mind?"

"Yeah, sure, of course." Robbie stepped aside.

Hayduke brushed past him. "You got a beer?"

"Sure." Robbie walked to the kitchen—aware of the stack of papers on the table—and got another beer from the fridge. He handed it to Hayduke in such a way that the young man turned away from the kitchen to take it.

"Hey, where's your pop?" Hayduke sucked the beer can and belched.

"I don't know. He went out into the Monument to look for you."

"Didn't find me. What did he want?"

"He was worried. I guess he was afraid that whoever killed Penelope and the others was coming after you next."

"Smith? You didn't hear? They busted that motherfucker this afternoon!" Hayduke held his beer aloft and howled. "About fucking time. That slimy bastard was defrauding the American people while Jacob Isaiah and Eleanor Barry were getting rich. I always knew this plot to build a resort out there in the goddamned Monument was a hoax."

"So, you're not worried?"

"No way. Smith did Penny and them others. It will come out in a matter of time."

"I guess so."

"Hey, can I use the pisser?"

"Yeah, sure."

Hayduke emptied the can into his mouth and then walked into the washroom, the can still clutched in his hand. As soon as he closed the door Robbie heard the water in the sink turn on. Robbie quickly gathered up the papers from the table. He looked around the room for a place to hide them. The water went off in the bathroom. He heard urinating in the toilet. Robbie opened the cupboard beneath the sink and stuffed the papers there next to the dish rack and cleaning products. He figured he had another twenty seconds or so before Hayduke was done with the toilet.

"Doing the dishes?" Hayduke was behind him. Robbie hadn't even heard the bathroom door open. He started to turn. The sound of urinating was louder. "Don't turn around." Hayduke's voice was different. He didn't affect the oafish tone that Robbie had become accustomed to.

"I'm just looking for a cloth to clean up—"

"Cut the bullshit, Rob. We both know what you've got in your hand. And I said don't turn around."

"Are you still in the bathroom?"

"Little trick with an empty beer can. Fill it up with water and balance it on the toilet seat. It sounds pretty convincing, doesn't it?" The sound stopped. Robbie could feel Hayduke behind him, could smell his thick odor and hear him breathing.

"Now, you're going to have a little nap." Robbie tried to turn and swing at the man, but Hayduke clamped a solid arm around him, pulling the smaller man into his grasp. Rob struggled, throwing his elbow into Hayduke's gut, then ribs. He pushed backwards, the kitchen table toppling over, but Hayduke pulled Robbie even tighter, his massive arm choking Pearson's windpipe. Then there was a cloth over Robbie's face; he struggled to breathe amid the sickly fumes. The room swam around him and then he lost consciousness.

39

KATIE RAIN STOOD IN FRONT of Silas Pearson's door. The rain drove down hard on the blacktop but under the awning of the second-storey rooms she was dry. She had determined that Silas's car wasn't in the parking lot, but there were lights on in the room, and she figured that Robbie was there. The BC license plates on his aging Tempo had been a giveaway. She rapped on the door and stood back out of habit. There was no answer. She knocked again, louder. Still nothing.

She pulled her phone out of her pocket and dialed a number. "Eugene, it's Rain. Where are you?"

"I'm at the BLM office."

She gave him an address. "I think we have a problem."

They met at the manager's office and Special Agent Nielsen produced his badge and asked for a key. Rain and Nielsen went back to the room. "What makes you think something's up?" asked Nielsen as they climbed the stairs.

"Robbie's vehicle is here but no one is answering. He drove it downtown earlier in the day and I assume he drove it back again. He isn't in the laundry or at the vending machines."

She knocked on the door for a third time. "FBI, open up," called Nielsen.

He slipped his sidearm from its holster and inserted the key in the lock. He opened the door and quickly entered. The room was empty. The kitchen table had been upended and a chair had toppled over backwards. There was an empty beer can on the floor and the room spelled faintly of the brew.

Nielsen quietly went to the bathroom and pushed the door open. Nothing but another beer can on the floor.

Katie looked around the room. She sniffed the air. "We have a problem."

"What?"

"You don't smell that?"

"A little like rubbing alcohol?"

"Chloroform."

Nielsen had his phone out and was dialing. "I need a serious incident response team at the following location."

GARFIELD COUNTY SHERIFF'S were the first to respond on the scene. The members of the FBI team who arrested Eleanor Barry arrived shortly after.

Nielsen had assembled them outside the door to Silas's motel room. "Here's the situation. We have the probable abduction of one Robert Pearson, white, male, twenty-four years old. Suspect is one Josh Charleston, AKA Hayduke. Ballistics analysis received earlier this evening suggests that Charleston is a person of interest in the murder of Penelope de Silva, the stepmother of the missing young man. Charleston is also a person of interest in at least two other murders, and maybe more. Assistant Special Agent in Charge Dwight Taylor has issued a nationwide APB for Charleston. We're going to coordinate with Kane County Sheriff's, the BLM, and state troopers. Our goal is to find Charleston and Pearson, pronto. We are also on the lookout for Pearson's father, who many of you know: Silas Pearson. He went out into the Monument this morning to look for Charleston and hasn't been seen since. At present we have no reason to believe that foul play is involved in his absence—he's likely just stuck somewhere in the rain—but let's see if we can't pick him up.

"We've spoken with the owner of the pizza place down the road, and we know that Pearson left there shortly after nine." Nielsen looked at his watch. "That means Charleston has got a two-and-a-half-hour jump on us. State troopers have got roadblocks on Highways 12, 22, 89, and 24 as well as I-15. Charleston is more likely to use gravel roads or Jeep trails for flight, so the BLM is providing maps of all the possible routes out of Escalante that he might have taken, and will provide officers and vehicles suitable to search those areas. Finally, we know he's armed and dangerous. Proceed with extreme caution. We'll have more resources in a few hours; Taylor is scrambling air recognizance out of Salt Lake City, but with the storm and the low ceiling it's going to be challenging to find him that way. This is a foot race, folks, and if we want to bring Pearson back alive, we've got to win it. Let's move."

40

A FLASH OF LIGHTNING ILLUMINATED the Straight Cliffs to the west of the Hole in the Rock Road, and a few seconds later thunder rolled across Ten Mile Flat. The glare from the lightning brightened the road in front of him for a moment. He could see clearly the way forward was no easier than the three miles he had already walked. The road was a quagmire of mud, a foot deep in places. When he had crossed it ten minutes earlier there had been two feet of water pooling in Cottonwood Wash.

Silas Pearson was soaked, shivering, and walking nearly blind through the downpour. Penelope's prized journal was stuffed under his shirt and kept mostly dry by his coat. He was caked in mud; he'd slipped twice near Halfway Hollow and was now dragging himself through the gloom. Rage fueled his march. He would have lain down and waited the storm out back at the campsite had it not been for the boiling anger he now felt. He had no idea where Hayduke had gone, but he knew that he had to get out of the Monument and if that meant walking all the way back to Escalante he would do it.

He had done it before. For almost five years he'd been tracking her last movements across the Colorado Plateau. It had all been for naught. He thought that she had gone off in search of sublime beauty and instead she had been killed in cold blood. And by this man, this caricature of an Edward Abbey persona, someone who Silas had come to trust, if only reluctantly.

Why had Hayduke spent so much of the last year and a half befriending him? Why had he invested so much time helping him find Penelope? And the others? Darcy McFarland and Kiel Pearce?

The answer seemed obvious now: deception. All this time Josh Charleston had been leading Silas away from the truth, not toward it. Silas wanted answers, and that desire kept him walking.

He had covered another slow mile and was trudging through standing water on the road from one of the forks of Harris Wash when he saw headlights in the distance.

He checked his watch. It was two in the morning. Who would be out in the Monument at that time of night? He slowed as the lights grew closer. Maybe Hayduke had changed his mind and returned. If the young man was coming back there was only one possible reason: to kill Silas.

Silas stepped off the road and ducked down behind a clump of rabbit brush. The headlights belonged to a heavy vehicle grinding through the muck in low range at five miles per hour. It *could* be Hayduke's Jeep.

When the vehicle was alongside Silas's hiding location, Silas could see the insignia on the door. Bureau of Land Management: the stewards of the Grand Staircase-Escalante National Monument. Silas jumped up and waved his arms and the vehicle came to a stop. The passenger window was rolled down.

"You Dr. Pearson?"

"Yeah!"

The door opened and a uniformed woman wearing a slicker stepped out of the vehicle. "Better hop in, we need to get you back to Escalante."

"I'm covered in mud."

"It will wash. Get in, we've got some news we need to discuss with you."

Silas got into the backseat of the pickup. The driver started the process of turning around on the mud-stricken road and the ranger twisted in her seat to look at Silas.

"I'll get right to the point, Dr. Pearson. Your son, Robert, has been abducted. We believe a man named Josh Charleston, who we understand to be an acquaintance of yours, is responsible. He's got a four-hour head start on us at this time. Is there anything you can tell us about Mr. Charleston that might help us find your son?"

Silas sat silently for a long time. Water ran from his hair down his face. He was streaked with mud.

"Dr. Pearson? Is there anything you can tell us?"

Silas told them about the game Charleston had introduced.

"*Hayduke Lives*? Jesus, that was a terrible book," the BLM ranger driving said.

"My son is now at the center of its plot."

"THIS MIGHT BE OF SOME help." Silas was in his hotel room with Eugene Nielsen and Katie Rain. The mobile command unit for the FBI was being established at the BLM headquarters just outside of town. Silas had quickly showered off most of the mud from the Monument and changed into dry clothing.

He placed Penelope's journal on the table in front of them. All three of them stared at it for a moment. "This is my wife's journal. It's a record of all the places that she visited in the Southwest. It's also a list of locations she hoped to include in a presidential proclamation to protect the American Southwest. She was going to call it the Edward Abbey National Monument."

Nielsen smirked. "That wouldn't have gone over all that well with the western delegation of Congress."

"Penelope was a pragmatist; she would have found a way to make it work."

"How do you think this might help?" asked Katie.

Silas flipped the journal open and pointed to the notes scribbled on the inside cover. There were water stains now, and the pages had started to buckle from the dampness. He tapped his finger on the marker-scrawled words *Call Hayduke*. "That's how I found him in the first place."

Nielsen pulled on a pair of latex gloves and spun the book around to look at it. He flipped open the first few pages and read them. He then went back to the front page and read the other notes jotted there.

"If I sent this to Quantico they could spend some time analyzing the handwriting, but I don't need to. This isn't how *you* found Hayduke; it's how *he* found *you*. This note—*Call Hayduke*—wasn't a note your wife wrote to remind herself to call her buddy. It was a note that *he* wrote inside the journal to get you to call him."

The color drained from Silas's face.

"Silas, how did you find this journal? Have you had it ever since your wife went missing?"

"No, I found it a year and a half ago." He told them the harrowing story of finding the journal hidden in Hatch Wash.

"So you thought Hayduke would be able to help you find your wife, and after you escaped with the journal, you called him up." Nielsen was flipping through the pages.

"That's right. I needed to find someone from Penelope's life before she disappeared that might help me locate her. I didn't even know this journal existed! It made me start to think: what else don't I know? Hayduke had so many answers."

"Lies, Dr. Pearson. Josh Charleston had so many lies."

"That's becoming plain now. Hayduke—he took Penelope's journal from her after he killed her."

"Dr. Pearson, we searched your home and it wasn't there. Where was it?"

"At my lawyer's; at Ken's place."

Nielsen nodded thoughtfully. "If we'd had this a year and a half ago—"

Rain put a hand on Nielsen's arm. "Eugene, not now."

Nielsen shrugged. "I'm going to get this up to Salt Lake. We have a forensic tech there who might be able to do some work with it. Is there anything else in it that might help?"

"This was all about the Colorado River," said Silas. "It was all about Glen Canyon Dam and Lake Powell. Penny, Darcy, Kiel, Tabby, and Josh, they were a team. They didn't work for any conservation group; they had a plan of their own. They wanted to drain Lake Powell." Silas told them everything he had learned. "They had photos—Tabby took them, he was a PI—of Smith with Eleanor Barry. They were . . . compromising. They would have thrown a monkey wrench in Smith's career; maybe kept him from winning his party's nomination for the big ticket. Penelope gave copies to the *Salt Lake Tribune* reporter Kresge but she wouldn't let him publish them. Then Kresge died in a car accident. Brake lines failed. Doesn't that sound like what happened to me on Comb Ridge last year?"

Both Rain and Nielsen nodded.

"I thought that Smith had them all killed."

"I can see why," said Rain. "But now you think that Hayduke killed them all?"

"Kresge is still up in the air," said Nielsen. "Our Provo office is going back over records of that accident we've obtained from the local sheriff's department. I like Hayduke for the others. Tabby is still officially missing, but Pearce and McFarland are in Hayduke's column."

"But the way all these people were killed was so different. Don't serial murders like to kill the same way over and over?"

"Hayduke is different, Silas. He's not a serial killer first and foremost. He's pathological. Likely a sociopath or even a psychopath, but he's not killing randomly. He's using whatever means he has most available when the opportunity arises. Where did Hayduke come up with a supply of chloroform?" asked Katie.

"I think I know. His parents are dentists. I bet he liberated some from them. They must have had a supply left over from when it was used during root canals. If you check I bet you'll find that some is missing," said Silas.

"We'll get someone to look into it. Right now our priority is getting your son back, Dr. Pearson."

That brought Silas back to the moment.

"Silas," said Rain. "Where do you think Hayduke is going?"

"I don't know. I doubt he's trying to get out of the country or anything like that. And I doubt he's going to Salt Lake or some other city. This guy really believes that he's George Washington Hayduke."

"You're a literature professor. Where would Hayduke take someone?"

Silas smiled wanly. "You know, before all of this with my wife, I hated Edward Abbey. Now I've read all of his books twenty times trying to figure out where my wife went missing. I know them pretty well. Or at least I thought I did. Turns out I didn't."

"You better hope you know them pretty well, Dr. Pearson, because right now we're in a race against time to find your son."

42

IT WAS AGREED THAT KATIE Rain would stay with Silas in his hotel room until an FBI technician could set up a phone trace on the landline into the room. They would wait to see if Hayduke called. Agent Nielsen left to go to the mobile command post at the BLM offices.

"Do you need anything?" Katie asked.

"Besides the obvious?"

"We'll get him back, Silas."

Silas just nodded. "I feel like an idiot."

"Don't—"

"He hoodwinked me."

"Not just you. All of us. We had him in our Monticello office last year, remember? We had his vehicle. I bet when we find that Jeep and measure the tires we'll get a match with the tracks that led up the Island in the Sky from Potash. Remember we found a half-dozen or so sets of tracks? I bet that Jeep is one of them. Don't beat yourself up. Taylor and Nielsen are good agents and they missed it too."

"I can't lose him, Katie. I need to call his mother. She's going to kill me."

"You need to keep your room phone line open." Katie dug out her cell. "Use my phone."

"I should be out there looking for him. I found him once tonight . . ." Silas looked at his watch. It was four in the morning. "Last night I mean. I can find him again."

"Silas, you need to stay put. You can't go running all over the place. If you do, we're going to have to divert resources from the search to find you. Do you understand?"

Silas reached his hand out for her cell. "I think I'll make the call from outside. The rain's slowing down. I do this outside, you won't have to listen to her yelling at me."

Silas walked to the door. It was cool outside and the desert smelled like rain. It was an odd juxtaposition. Silas opened the phone function on Katie's iPhone and queued up the keypad. He noted on the desktop that there were unread text messages.

He dialed the familiar number of his ex-wife in Vancouver, Canada. She answered after three rings. "Who is this?"

"Terri, it's Silas. Yes, I know; I'm aware of what time it is. Listen, stop for a minute. We need to talk."

HE STOOD ON the balcony of the second floor of the motel for a long time after he hung up the phone. Just what he needed: his ex-wife would be on the first flight into Salt Lake that morning. But could he blame her? He knew that he would do the same thing.

Dawn was approaching and Silas hadn't slept. Somewhere, out there in the desert, there was a madman holding his son hostage. He *hoped* he was still holding his son. What did Hayduke want? In the sequel to *The Monkey Wrench Gang*, called *Hayduke Lives*, four crusaders from the first novel reunite to carry on in a comical parody of their first more genuine adventures. Abbey had as much as admitted in his published journals—*Confessions of a Barbarian*—that he wrote it to make some fast cash for his family after he had been told he was dying. Silas couldn't blame him for that.

What had Hayduke meant by "game"?

Katie Rain's cell phone buzzed. He thought it might be Terri calling back, but it was a text message. Silas looked back toward the room, then opened the message.

You haven't responded, the text read. It was from a Utah area code.

Silas thumbed down to the message before it in chronological order and read it.

On your feet! It's Hayduke, Dr. Rain. This message is for Silas. I fucked up his phone and I'm betting that you two are getting cozy right now. Here are my instructions. Neither you or Silas are to inform the FBI or any other law enforcement agencies of this message, or involve them in any way. If you do, I will kill Robbie Pearson. Text me when you're ready to start our adventure.

Silas felt all of the blood drain from his face. His hands began to shake. He tried to use the keyboard on the phone's surface to craft a response. After several tries he got something typed.

This is Silas. I'm ready. He hit send.

He waited a moment and another message appeared on the phone.

It took you long enough. I thought I might have to just kill Rob now instead of playing our game. The Chase Begins: "The bridge still stands, apparently essentially intact, arched above the flood, above the trench of the darkening canyon." You'll find what you are looking for there. No FBI or Robbie dies.

SILAS STARED AT the phone in his hand. He knew the reference. Hayduke was directing him to the bridge over White Canyon. The line was from *The Monkey Wrench Gang*. The White Canyon Bridge was the Gang's final target. They had intended to melt the girders that supported the bridge, but failed, and ended up on the run from the San Juan County Search and Rescue Team. The bridge was located at the northeast end of Lake Powell where the Dirty Devil, White, and Colorado Rivers all converged. It was at least a three-hour drive. Hayduke had started both messages—*On Your Feet* and *The Chase Begins*—with chapter headings from his namesake's book.

The FBI, the Kane, Grand, and Garfield County Sheriff's Departments, state troopers, even the Bureau of Land Management were already involved. By morning the Park Service would be flying over Grand Canyon, Bryce Canyon, Capital Reef, and Canyonlands National Parks. Hayduke must know this. He'd be taking precautions to stay off the main roads and cover his tracks.

Silas leaned on the railing. The door behind him opened and Katie said his name. He turned to look at her. "How'd that go?"

"About as well as can be expected. She's coming out."

"I don't blame her."

"This will be over soon, right?" Silas felt as if he might throw up.

"I don't know, Silas. Agent Nielsen is one of the best at this sort of thing. He's had lots of experience. And Taylor will be here in a couple of hours. We'll find Robbie."

"Alive?"

"Alive."

"I need to take another quick shower. I still feel as if I'm covered in mud."

"I can watch the phone while you do that."

"Could I have just a few minutes alone?"

"I don't think that's a good idea. If Hayduke calls, I need to be listening in."

"Just a few minutes."

She hesitated. "Alright. I'll go and change too and be right back up. Can I take my phone now?"

"Rob's mother said she would call me back when she's got her ticket booked. Do you mind?"

"That's my personal phone, so no problem. Silas, we're *going* to get Robbie back."

Silas forced a thin smile and nodded. "I'll leave the door unlocked."

Katie left and Silas slipped into his room and closed the door. He grabbed a dry jacket and a few other pieces of clothing and jammed them in his pack. He stuffed Katie's phone into his pocket. He then took Robbie's keys from the dresser. He opened the cabinet under the sink to look for a water bottle. The stack of papers that Robbie had hidden there were on the shelf. He picked them up and looked at the first page or two. His heart sank further. He stuffed the papers in his bag.

Silas quickly left the room, closing the door quietly behind him. He went to the far end of the catwalk and went down the stairs to where Robbie's car was parked. He opened the door and sat in the front seat, breathing out as he did. The rain had stopped but the world was still glistening with moisture. He slipped the keys into the ignition and turned the engine over.

As he did, the passenger door opened abruptly and Katie Rain sat down in the vehicle. "Going somewhere?" She was smiling, but there was an edge to her voice.

"I was heading over to the BLM office."

"Give me my phone, Silas." He handed her the phone. She scrolled through the conversation with Hayduke. Silas stared straight ahead as Katie read the messages.

"You know where he's talking about?"

"Yeah, it's the bridge over the White Canyon."

"This line, it's from one of Edward Abbey's books, isn't it?"

He told her about what Hayduke had told him out at Devil's Garden, and about the scene in *The Monkey Wrench Gang* that takes place at the White River Bridge.

"You go off and try and confront this guy on your own and you're going to get your son and yourself killed."

"He said no FBI."

"Of course he said no FBI. Everybody who ever kidnaps anybody says no FBI. But the only way we get Robbie back is to narrow the search grid and find a way to negotiate with Hayduke. This information," she held her phone up, "would help Nielsen and Taylor do just that."

"He's not going to be there. He's too smart. He's been planning this." Silas pulled out the papers he'd taken from under the sink.

"What's that?"

"They were in the room. Robbie must have hidden them before Hayduke grabbed him. It's the research that he was doing today. These are postings from a blog set up by some guys who created something called the Hayduke Trail. It's a rugged back-country hiking route that circles the Southwest following locations from *The Monkey Wrench Gang*." Silas riffled through the pages. "Josh Charleston has been posting on it for the last couple of months. He's been hiking all over the various sections of the trail here in the Escalante and down into Canyonlands, asking questions about distances and road access. Look, Robbie highlighted this section where Josh asks *Can I get from Hite into the Maze district on the old Jeep trail that Hayduke took in* The Monkey Wrench Gang?"

"Silas, this doesn't mean he was planning this."

"I think it does. Look here; Robbie found this posting: *Time to play a game of Hayduke Lives*. Charleston—Hayduke—posted that two weeks ago! That was just after we found where Penelope was murdered. I think he knew that you guys would eventually draw the line back to him. There was nothing he could do at that time to steer us away from the evidence. He was the one who firebombed my store, and he stole Penelope's journal later that night to try and erase the evidence that he had planted it for me to find in the first place. He'd already been planning an escape route at that point, and when I didn't die in the store fire, he kicked it into high gear."

"Why not just run? He could have slipped across the border into Mexico and been long gone."

"I don't know. He's crazy? He *believes* he *is* Hayduke?"

"If you're right, if he has been planning this out, what happens next? He's given you a destination. He's using *The Monkey Wrench Gang* as some sort of guidebook to draw you in. What's next?"

Silas pressed his fingers to his forehead. He turned and leaned over the seat and grabbed the worn copy of the novel he had given Robbie to read. He handed Katie the paperback. "If I'm correct, he's going to head toward Canyonlands. He might try and follow the old Jeep trails above Cataract Canyon. I don't even know if they are passable. But maybe he's got something else planned. In *Hayduke Lives* the character blows up a power plant. Josh could be planning anything. The only way I'm going to find out is to go to the White River Bridge."

"Taylor can—"

"No he can't! Not now. He can't do anything to get my son back that I can't do alone. Hayduke sees the FBI coming, he's going to kill Robbie just like he killed those others and the game will be over. Hayduke *lives*. Get it?"

Rain sat silently next to Silas for a long time. "Alright, here's the deal. I'm coming with you. We go to the White River Bridge and find out what Hayduke wants. Then you and I call Taylor and tell him what's going on. Deal?"

"What if I say no?"

"Then I arrest you."

"Then I guess we have a deal."

"And we take my truck. This old jalopy isn't going to get us far."

43

THEY DROVE IN SILENCE FOR the first hour, passing through Boulder and taking the Burr Trail over the Circle Cliffs and into Capital Reef National Park. Silas sat behind the wheel of her Toyota Tundra while Katie sat speed-reading *The Monkey Wrench Gang* in the passenger seat. Silas had given her his copy from the portable Abbey library he had in the hotel room. The sun rose as they were approaching Highway 276 south of the Henry Mountains. The first light of morning reflected off the previous evening's rain-soaked desert. If Silas hadn't been in a race to save his oldest son from a killer, he might have even found the dawn beautiful.

"What do you think we're going to find when we get there?" Katie asked as they turned onto Highway 95. She was reading the final chapters of the book.

"I don't know. It depends on what Josh thinks the end game will be."

They crossed the bridge over the Dirty Devil River and then the Colorado itself.

"That's the turn-off for Hite," said Silas. "The White Canyon Bridge is just up ahead." He started to slow the truck. They drove onto the bridge, the only vehicle in sight. Below them, the stagnant waters of the White River were hemmed between the sandstone walls of its canyon.

Silas stopped the truck in the middle of the bridge and got out. Katie did too.

The morning was cool and still. The light on the canyon walls glowed with a rosy countenance. Katie scanned the surrounding landscape.

Silas paced up and down the driving lane. "In the book the Gang tries to burn through the bridge's super-structure with thermite. They placed a barrel of it at one end of the bridge and lit it on fire and watched it burn down through the asphalt, but nothing happened. It made a big hole in the road but the bridge's girders remained intact. It was a turning point, because shortly afterwards the San Juan Search and Rescue Team got after them and the chase was on."

"How did the Search and Rescue Team find them? I didn't get that when I read the book just now."

"Bishop Love, the head of the Team, had a real hate on for Hayduke. Hayduke had given him the slip a week before and humiliated him so the Bishop was out to get him. Right before they did the bridge job Hayduke took out a few bulldozers over by Hite. Drove them over the cliff. Big explosion."

"Not the actions of someone trying to be inconspicuous."

"Inconspicuous isn't a word a character like Hayduke understands."

Katie leaned on the railing and looked down into the canyon. "So it was hubris that did in Hayduke and his friends."

"I think so. How is that going to help me get my son back?"

"It's something to keep in mind. You've spent a lot more time around Josh Charleston than I have, but it seems to me hubris is something this young man has in abundance. Whether he comes by it naturally, or maybe he's adopted it as part of his persona, he seems to display it with startling regularity."

"So Josh said we'd find something here that would lead us to Robbie. Do you see anything?"

Silas removed a pair of binoculars from his pack and scanned the length of the bridge. It was a simple, inelegant structure with supports anchored into the canyon walls at either end and a plain flat deck that spanned the gorge below. He walked to the end closest to the Hite marina where the Monkey Wrench Gang had done their work.

Katie followed him, scanning the surrounding bluffs for signs of trouble.

As he neared the end of the bridge something caught Silas's eye and he picked up his pace, breaking into a run for a few strides. Katie hurried after him. Silas stopped twenty feet from the end of the bridge. On the edge of the bridge, secured to the railing, was a metal ammo can.

"Silas, don't touch that."

"It's got to be from him."

"I'm sure it is, but you don't know what it is. It could be an explosive."

"He's not going to blow me up, not yet at least. The game is just beginning."

"And you're going to play along?"

"What choice do I have?"

"You can let me call Taylor and put his people on this. It's what they do; they're good at this."

"This is my son's life we're talking about. Do you think that Josh won't kill him at the first sight of trouble? Then he just disappears into the Canyons, forever."

"Even Hayduke couldn't disappear, not forever."

"Yeah, well, I don't particularly care what happens to Hayduke—to Josh—but I do care what happens to Robbie. You can stand back if you think it's a bomb. I'm going to open it." He waited and when Rain made no move to step back he knelt down on the ground and snapped open the box.

44

THE STURDY METAL CAN SNAPPED open. No bomb detonated. Silas breathed out and Katie seemed to relax for a moment. Inside was a folded sheet of paper.

Silas opened the note and read, "*Because the Maze is a dead end, Doc. The end of the road. The big jump-off. Nobody ever goes to the Maze.*"

"I just read that!" exclaimed Katie.

"Yeah, it's from *The Monkey Wrench Gang*. Jesus, I'm starting to hate that book all over again."

"You think he's taken Robbie into the Maze?"

"I think it's obvious what he's doing. He's following the path that the Gang took during the final chase in the book. Hayduke is leading us into the Maze."

"To what end? Hayduke dies at the end of the book."

"Didn't you read the epilogue?"

"I ran out of time."

"Hayduke *lives*. That's the whole point. *That's* the game he's playing. He's cornered. We know he killed Penelope. So he's making a run for it, using Robbie as both bait and cover."

"Why not just run?"

"You ask that as if we were dealing with a sane person. Why kill Penny? Why kill Darcy and Kiel and likely Tabby Dingwall too?"

"This note—do you know where this takes place in the book?" Katie was scanning the landscape once again.

"I sure do. Just back up the road we came down. There's an old Jeep trail that leads along the plateau above the Colorado River for thirty miles and ends up in an area called the Fins. Then the Maze."

"In the book, doesn't Hayduke get in a gunfight with a whole bunch of law enforcement types?"

"Yeah, so?"

"If Josh is trying to recreate the end of the book for himself, then maybe that's what he wants."

"To get in a gunfight? Look, that turned out alright for the character Hayduke in the book. That book was set in the 1970s and Edward Abbey didn't really have a good grasp of what a tactical team would be using as weapons. He had guys firing shotguns out of helicopters."

"I see what you mean. Taylor's Critical Incident Response Group would be geared up. MP5 sub-machine guns, CAR-15s, HK33s and M40 sniper rifles."

"Hayduke is a vet. He's got to know that."

"Standard procedure is for the nearest SWAT team to be scrambled whenever the FBI is lead on a situation like this. From here, that would be Salt Lake. But the resident office in Monticello has tactical capability as well. My bet is that a team is already in place, on standby. A gunfight with these guys is going to be a very one-sided affair."

"He's trying to control the situation," Silas said as they half-ran back to Katie's truck. He held the note up. "He's leading us to him. He wants to act out the end of the game. He can't control a gunfight with the guys you're describing. That's why he's said no FBI. He knows it won't be a bunch of weekend warriors and small-town sheriff's deputies he's dealing with."

"Our FBI team can be discreet."

"How? The place he's leading us—likely to Lizard Rock—it's out in the middle of nowhere. You have to drive in, on a Jeep trail, and it's going to be pretty obvious if a couple of big GMC Yukons pull up. He'll be watching. What I'm starting to realize is that he's *always* been watching. He's been watching me all along."

Katie got into the vehicle and turned it around in the middle of the bridge. "Where am I going?" She turned on the dashboard-mounted GPS unit. She hit a few buttons, programming the unit, and the device started to send and receive data.

"Back the way we came. On our right."

"What did you mean, he's always been watching?"

"When I started to have my dreams, where Penny was leading me places, to bodies, that's when *he* showed up. I must have tripped some wire he had set. Maybe he was watching the newspapers for my name and after the body in Sleepy Hollow, my name was in the paper a lot. That's when he showed up. I remember the day. I was up in the La Sals and there he was. He made it seem so . . . coincidental, us just running into each other. There, that's it, on the right."

Katie slowed the vehicle and turned into the dirt track.

"Just stop a minute. Let's look around."

Katie stopped the vehicle. The dirt road was wet, the red clay and sand slick. Silas stepped out of the truck. Katie took the binoculars and scanned the cliffs and buttes that surrounded them. The morning sun was higher now, the shadows still draped like dark cloth over the red rock.

"You see anything?" Silas asked as he searched the area around the road.

"Nope. You?"

"Nope. Wait . . ."

Silas set off into the rocks.

"What do you see?" Katie was rushing to keep up.

"Another goddamned ammo box."

"Where? Oh, I see it."

Perched on top of a boulder, twenty yards from the road, the ammo can was painted bright orange. Silas approached it and looked around. He could hear a few birds calling from a patch of cliff rose, and somewhere above a broad-winged bird of prey circled. Otherwise the desert seemed empty. He popped the ammo can open. There was another note.

Thirty-five miles to Lizard Rock was all it said.

"Son of a bitch. He *is* leading us to the Maze."

"You called it right. Listen, Silas—"

"No goddamned FBI, Katie."

"I'm FBI, Silas."

Silas looked at her. "You're . . . different."

"You think that's going to matter to him?"

"I don't know. I don't care. I need you. And you were invited. He as much as said so in his text message."

"And I'm here. But we've got to get help. We're walking straight into a trap. We know where he's going and we know what he's going to do. We have the advantage."

"We don't have shit! What we have are notes written by a lunatic quoting from a book. I think they might mean he wants us to go to Lizard Rock, but who knows? I don't know for sure. Josh is insane. He could change the story. He could do anything. One wrong move and my son gets killed. So no FBI!" Silas still had Katie's phone. He looked at the screen. There was no service, and no messages waiting. He put it on the ground and, with his boot, stomped on it. "That settles it."

Katie's face remained calm. "Silas, I can turn this truck around right now—"

"And what? Leave me here? Leave Rob at the mercy of that madman?"

"I can drive into Hite, phone Taylor, and have him put a Hostage Rescue Team in play."

"You'd be killing my son."

"What do you think is going to happen when we get to this Lizard Rock? You think Josh is just going to hand out party hats and say that the game is over? No, he's going to kill Rob and then he's going to kill you and me."

"You won't let that happen. I won't let that happen."

"So what's your plan? You going to outflank him? With what? What are you going to use to get the jump on him?"

"You're armed."

"Sure. I've got my sidearm. I haven't shot it outside the range in ten years. And what do you have?"

"Charm and good looks?"

"You looked in the mirror lately, Silas? Seriously, what have you got?"

They were standing face to face in the middle of the road. Silas had sweat forming along his prickly hairline. His eyes were red and his face, though sunburnt, seemed splotchy and pale. "I know the country. I know the book. I know what should happen. If he's going to play it out just like in the book I think we can flank him, or whatever you call it."

Rain smiled and shook her head. "Bones. All I wanted to do was look at bones. But no, I have to go and fall . . . I have to go and take a shine to you. A scruffy professor out wandering around the desert looking for his wife. Alright, genius, what's your plan?"

"This is four-wheel drive, right?"

GUNSIGHT BUTTE, TEAPOT Rock, the Red Cove, the Golden Stairs: the land unfolded before them. Katie drove over the double-track road, Silas scanning the horizon. From time to time they stopped to inspect the road; sure enough there were signs that at least one vehicle had traveled this way since the end of the storm.

"Could these be from Josh's Jeep?" Silas asked.

Rain shrugged. "Could be. I don't know this stuff. Nielsen knows his tire tracks."

"We better keep moving. We're ten miles from Lizard Rock."

"I don't know how you're holding out, Silas, but this girl has got to pee." Silas nodded and stepped out of the vehicle. She waited until he was gone and then disappeared behind a boulder and came back a minute later.

"You got anything to eat in your truck?" asked Silas.

"I got a box of granola bars."

"Sold."

"It's going to cost you."

"What?"

"A new phone."

"Sorry about that."

"Not as sorry as you're going to be when you find out what they cost."

They drove on. The sun reached high noon. In the middle of October it still cast long shadows over the naked stone. The Flint Trail, the main road to the edge of the Maze, was used more regularly. "There's likely to be other people in the Maze right now. It's not like when Abbey wrote about the place," said Silas. "In October other folks head in there to use the Jeep trails and hike and explore. It's too hot in July and August, but September and October are perfect."

"I hope Josh doesn't get antsy if he runs into some tourist from Ohio."

"That's Lizard Rock, there on the horizon. Stop here."

Katie pulled up next to a large boulder on the side of the road.

"I'm guessing we're going to find another message at Lizard Rock. From there, I think he's going to lead us out to Standing Rock and then on foot to Horse Canyon."

"And then what?"

"Well, that's the end of the road. In the book, Horse Canyon is where Hayduke got into the gunfight and faked his own death. Robbie and I were in Horse Canyon in September. We came at it from the Green River side of things. I don't see anything," Silas scanned the horizon with Katie's binoculars. "We'd better get a move on."

They drove on. Lizard Rock loomed closer. All around the landscape was composed of vertical outcrops of red and white sandstone, but Lizard Rock was singular. Rising nearly a hundred feet in a narrow spire, and topped with a bulbous head that looked like the mouth of a lizard, the rock was a landmark on the Flint Trail and a magnet for climbers. Silas breathed a sigh of relief that nobody was on the tower that afternoon.

They slowed on the road and Silas was out of the truck before Katie had stopped. He was looking for another ammo box. He circled the tower once and, finding nothing, circled again. Katie searched along the roadside, looking in the rabbit brush and saltbush.

"There's nothing here!" Silas was panting, more with panic than fatigue.

"He said Lizard Rock, right?"

Silas took the note out. "It says *Thirty-five miles to Lizard Rock.* It's a line from *The Monkey Wrench Gang*, when Seldom Seen Smith is explaining to Bonnie how far they are from their destination. It's obvious, isn't it?"

They walked in opposite directions around the rock but found nothing. They stopped near the road at the crude trail register the Park Service had put up. Silas leaned on it, dread spreading across his face. Then his face brightened.

"What? What is it?"

Silas opened the trail register's lid and hurriedly pulled out the notebook there. He flipped to the final page. There was an entry in the same juvenile handwriting he first saw in his wife's journal a year and a half ago. "*The ultimate world . . . the final world of meat, flood, fire, water, rock, wood, sun, wind, sky, night, cold, dawn, warmth, life . . . and loneliness . . ."*

"What does that mean?"

Silas was silent for a moment. "It's another line from the book. Remember? When Hayduke and Smith are at the end of the chase scene, trying to wait out the National Guard near Standing Rock. It's the end of the line. It's the last jump-off. It's Hayduke's last stand."

KATIE DROVE THROUGH the mid-afternoon sun. The Flint Trail rolled across the plateau; the canyons branched off from this high divide and fell into dark, sculpted defiles on either side of them. Far in the distance the red walls of the Island in the Sky, forty miles away and on the other side of the Green River, reflected the glow of autumn. Behind them the Orange Cliffs were backlit by the failing sun. The world was still and silent except the deep growl of the truck passing over the landscape.

There was a loud bang, and another. Silas ducked and Katie hunched behind the wheel. Two more loud bangs and the vehicle ground to a halt. Silas reached for the door handle.

"Wait!" shouted Rain.

"That was the tires—"

"I know. But that wasn't a sharp rock on the road that blew them out." She unholstered her sidearm and opened the door, ducking down behind it as she got out. Silas did the same. He could smell rubber. All four tires were flat.

"Jesus Christ," Silas muttered. "Caltrops."

"What are you talking about?"

"Caltrops. They're all over the road."

"Did Josh put these here?"

"Yeah. It's another thing from the book, remember? Doc used them to slow down the Search and Rescue Team. But that was supposed to be back on the White Canyon Bridge."

"He's changing the narrative."

"What else is he going to change?"

"Silas, I really think—"

"Listen, Katie, I'm not calling in Taylor. We can't now anyway. We're committed."

She was silent. He could hear her breathing on the other side of the vehicle. "Alright. Let's gear up. How far to Standing Rock?"

"Less than a mile. If he sticks to the narrative in the book, it will be another few miles out onto the mesa to Horse Canyon."

"Get your gear then. Let's go."

EACH CARRIED A light pack. Katie had removed the dash-mounted GPS and stowed it in her bag. They left the road. Silas argued that there might be more notes, or messages, but Katie countered that the message might come in the form of an ambush. "As long as Josh is changing the game plan, then so should we. Let's get off the road and find some cover to move under." They walked along the narrow plateau overlooking the folds and fins in the earth called the Maze as the sun sank toward the horizon.

"Alright," said Silas, watching Standing Rock from behind some low brush. "This is where we split up."

"Silas, are you sure about this?"

"No. But we've got to interrupt his plan. We can't let him get Robbie out to Horse Canyon. If he does, we're going to run out of options. Listen, I'm sorry to have dragged you into this. I mean, all of it. It's dangerous, and it's out of control. I know that."

"Well, when I helped you look for Penelope last fall, out on the Island in the Sky, I will admit I didn't see this coming."

"We get through this, I'll make it up to you."

"You're going to invite me over for a Hungry Man frozen dinner, are you?"

"Funny. I mean it, Katie—"

"Alright, enough. Let's go get your son back."

She unfolded the map he had given her and studied it for a minute. Smiling at him, she kissed him on the grizzled cheek. "It's going to be alright," she said, and then was gone.

He watched her trot off toward Standing Rock, hunched low, her pistol held close to her side, watching the horizon for signs of trouble. He felt an ominous sense of déjà vu.

"I'LL BE FOUR, maybe five days."

"Where are you heading this time?"

"I haven't figured that out yet. There are a lot of variables."

"You're the only person I know who has variables when it comes to backpacking. Can't you just decide on a hike and then do it?"

"It's not just a hike, Silas."

"I know, Penny. It's never just a hike with you."

"You say that like it's a bad thing. This is important to me. If you came with me sometime, you'd understand."

"I'll come sometime. It's just that right now it's the end of term and I've got a hundred papers to grade. If you'd schedule these things when I'm not busy with school—"

"Silas, the desert is hot in the summertime and snowy at Christmas. There's a reason I hike in the spring and the fall."

"Are you going to call me when you know where you're going?"

She kissed him on the forehead. "It will be within a day of Moab, one way or another."

He looked up from his papers. "There's a lot of country within a day of Moab."

"I know, isn't it wonderful?"

45

STANDING ROCK WAS ANOTHER PHALLIC spire in a land of pillars. Silas stood on the road, his hands at his sides, trying to look unthreatening. The sun was low on the horizon and long shadows drew away from the naked stone as if the skin of light that stretched over the world was being pulled taut by an invisible hand.

He carefully circled the column of stone. There was a breeze blowing across the desert and he could smell the sweet fragrance of sage. In the distance the La Sal Mountains, always his compass, glowed in the late afternoon light. There was fresh snow on their summits; another year come and gone.

He had checked the register at the end of the road and there was no message from Josh. There was no ammo box containing a line of prose from Edward Abbey. Just stillness; just silence, only the wind and the occasional croak of raven.

"Hayduke!" he called.

There was no answer.

"Josh, I'm here. I want my son!"

Nothing. He closed his eyes and felt the wind gently touch his face.

Then there was a noise. It was like the sound of a rock being dropped on the sand floor of a wash. He tensed. He turned to look around himself. All that existed was the naked earth. From Standing Rock to the Chocolate Drops—pillars of muddy brown stone beyond the canyons of the Maze—to Elaterite Butte on the horizon, nothing moved.

"Hayduke!"

"I'm right here, Silas."

Silas spun around but there was no one there. He took a few tentative steps toward the pillar of stone. "Where?"

"Here." Josh Charleston's voice seemed to float on the wind.

"Robbie? You alright?"

"He's fine." Hayduke was above him, standing at the base of the chimney of stone, high on the talus cone that formed at the sheer rock's base. The sun was behind Josh so Silas had to shield his eyes to see him. His son was there too, bound and gagged, silent. He looked haggard, his hair standing on end, one of his eyes swollen with bruising. Hayduke had his revolver in his right hand.

"I'm here, Josh—"

"It's Hayduke, for fuck's sake!"

"I'm here, Hayduke. Now, what do you want?"

"I want to end the game."

"Then let's talk about how we do that."

"You know how this ends."

"It doesn't have to. I've done what you asked. I'm here alone—"

Hayduke interrupted him with laughter that sounded like a bark.

"I'm here alone, no FBI, just like you said. Let Robbie go and you and me, we can go out to Horse Canyon and write a new ending to the story."

"Like what?" Hayduke was walking over the rough terrain toward Silas, pushing Robbie along as he did. "What's the new ending? Everybody lives happily ever after? I don't think ol' Cactus Ed would have liked that."

"But they did—everybody lived."

Hayduke was in front of him now. Silas looked Robbie over. He was bruised and bloody. He had a gash along his hairline above his left temple and his face was black and blue. Silas's eyes locked on his son's. He tried to convey that everything would be okay while Robbie seemed to be saying something else entirely.

"Let Rob go; he's not part of this story."

"I thought we'd use him as the scarecrow that goes down into the flood. You know, the one that Hayduke dresses up and throws down into the canyon to fool everybody into thinking that he's really dead?"

"I don't think that's a good idea." Sweat was beading on Silas's forehead. He pushed it away with the back of his hand. "Let Robbie go and you and I can go out to Horse Canyon and just talk this through."

"Talk? Talk? That's all you ever want to do! No fucking action, man. Penelope was the same in the end. Same goddamned thing. All talk. No action. We never could all get together on that one."

"What are you talking about?"

"It's from the book; Smith says that, right here, right fucking here, in the book. *We never could all get together on that one.* When he leaves Hayduke. When he walks away in the rain. Walks all the way back up the Flint Trail. Ten miles in the rain."

"Get together on what?"

"On the fucking dam."

"What are you talking about? Listen, I don't care what's happened before. I just want Robbie back." Silas shifted nervously.

"Did you like my notes? They led you right here."

"Yes, very clever."

"I thought you would like them. You say you hate him, but nobody knows Abbey the way you do."

"Jo . . . Hayduke, where is this all going?"

"You know where it's going!"

"Let's just be calm. Hayduke could have walked away. Why don't we rewrite the ending?"

"He was desperate."

"But you're not. It's just us. You could leave Robbie here, walk to wherever you left your Jeep, and nobody would ever find you. I'd tell them you'd gone to Canada."

Hayduke stiffened. He pushed the pistol into the side of Robbie's head. Rob winced and Silas's face registered panic. "You're a filthy stinking liar, you know that, Silas?"

"I wouldn't tell anybody."

"You weren't alone out here. You brought the girl."

"What do you—?"

"The girl. The FBI woman. Rain. You brought her."

"What have you done?"

"I took care of things."

"Josh, what have you done?"

"Let's just say your plan to catch Hayduke failed. I slipped the net."

"I just want my son back—please?"

Hayduke pressed the barrel of the heavy revolver into the side of Robbie's head. He thumbed the hammer but didn't cock the pistol. With a violent surge he swung the butt of the pistol into the young man's temple and Silas heard the crack; Robbie crumpled to the ground. Silas rushed forward but before he reached his son Josh raised the weapon and pointed it at Silas's head. "Stop!"

Silas skidded to a stop as Hayduke, his face twisted and mad, rushed at him. In a second Hayduke was on him, swinging the heavy pistol, the weapon clipping Silas in the face. Blood bloomed there. Silas stopped, looking at his son on the ground.

"Now, Dr. Pearson, let's finish up this little game of ours, shall we?"

46

"I'M NOT GOING WITH YOU, Hayduke." Silas stood looking at Josh Charleston, standing before him, ragged, sweating, and wild. Josh's extended arm still held his .357 Magnum pointed at Silas's forehead.

"You and I are going to march out to the end of this plateau and we're going to put a final exclamation point on this whole fucking business. Now get moving!"

"I'm not leaving Robbie. And Katie? Where is she?"

Hayduke swung the pistol and the barrel smashed into Silas's face. More blood painted the red earth of the desert. Silas spit a stream of saliva and blood onto the ground. "What was this all about? Were you in love with my wife, is that it? But she wouldn't have you, so you killed her?"

"It had nothing to do with that."

"Then what?"

"I know this is the part of the story where the hero gets the villain to confess to his motivations right before he's rescued and saved from oblivion, but as you can see," Hayduke gestured with his pistol to the empty landscape all around, "that's not going to happen."

"You said you couldn't all get together; did you mean about the dam?"

"It was always about the dam, you stupid fuck. Now, get on your goddamned feet and walk."

Silas sat down in the sand, his hand covering the wound on his cheek, blood leaking between his fingers. He leaned over and spit again. He had to brace himself with his hand to keep from passing out.

Hayduke took another step forward. He was standing over Silas now. Silas looked up at the young man. "I thought you were helping me."

"You were wrong. If you won't walk out to Horse Canyon then we'll just have to be satisfied with ending the story here." He pressed the pistol to Silas's forehead.

The desert for a hundred miles around Silas was silent. It rang in his ears. Even the wind seemed to have been sucked from the landscape. Where moments before he had heard birdsong at the end of the day, now there was nothing. He felt alone. Everything he loved was gone and he was staring into the oblivion of a madman's gun.

"Fuck you, Josh. You were a pathetic Hayduke."

"Feels good to get that out?"

Silas closed his eyes. Hayduke thumbed the hammer on the heavy pistol.

Even in the perfect silence of the Canyonlands, Silas didn't hear the shot.

47

ROBBIE'S HANDS WERE BOUND BY duct tape behind his back, which made sitting in the passenger seat of the Jeep both uncomfortable and awkward. The effects of the chloroform had worn off hours before, but his head still ached from where Josh had hit him. They were driving along a rough road—really little more than a trail—out into the heart of the desert. All around them the land was circled by cliffs and in the distance he could see the snow-capped mountains close to his father's house in the Castle Valley. Hayduke drove in silence.

They followed the road past a series of pillar-like rocks. At one point Josh stopped the Jeep, got out, and removed a box from the back of the vehicle. Robbie tried to turn his head to watch what he was doing, but he was stiff and he couldn't see the man from where he was sitting. When Josh got back in the Jeep he was smiling.

"Why are you doing this?" Robbie asked.

"I thought that would be pretty obvious to a smart guy like you."

"I get it that you're using me as bait. That much is clear. But why? What did my father ever do to you? I thought you were . . . friends?"

"We were never friends. He was using *me* to find Penelope."

"But you killed Penelope. And the others. Did you kill Tabby Dingwall?"

Josh smiled again. It wasn't the wolfish grin he had affected as the personification of Hayduke but instead was sly and menacing.

"Where are we going?"

"All the way to the end; all the way to the end."

"The end of what? The road?"

"All the way to the end of the story."

"What are you talking about?"

"You and I are going to be playing the role of Hayduke. You'll be the scarecrow and I'll be, well, me."

"I haven't read the book," Robbie lied. "If you want me to play along you're going to have to fill me in."

"Jesus Christ. At the end of *The Monkey Wrench Gang* Hayduke tries to get at a food cache the Gang has stashed at Standing Rock, but the National Guard has set up a camp there. He gets spotted and runs all the way out onto the neck of stone that overlooks Horse Canyon. It's a long fucking way, and I always did wonder what Abbey was thinking when he wrote that . . . But fuck it; he runs all the way out and hides in a crack in the rock. There's nowhere else to go. And then the Guard shows up and there's a big shootout. Hayduke even shoots down a helicopter! But he's trapped, so he dresses up a shrub in his clothing and uses it as a scarecrow. It gets the hell shot out of it, and falls down into a huge flood in Horse Canyon. That's going to be you. I get to escape."

"You're insane. It isn't even raining."

"Not anymore."

"Who plays the National Guard in your little story?"

"That's where your old man comes in."

"It's not going to work. My dad couldn't hit the broad side of a barn with a cannon. And he's not going to let you lure him all the way out to Horse Canyon."

"Then we'll have to resort to plan B. I just shoot you both in the head and disappear down into the Canyons."

Robbie was shaking his head. "Why did you kill Penelope?"

Hayduke pounded his hand on the steering wheel. "That bitch. She went off the reservation." Robbie waited for more, but Josh seemed lost in thought.

"She betrayed you?"

"She betrayed Glen Canyon. She betrayed the Colorado River. She betrayed us all."

"This is linked to the blackmail of Senator Smith."

"We had a plan. Use what we had to stop Smith from changing the Colorado River Compact. Once that was done, we would press him and others to decommission the dam. It's fucking useless right now; all it does is trap more and more silt. Another twenty years and it will be clogged with mud. So we tear it down. Blast the fucker right out of the canyon. But Penny backed out. She got cold feet or maybe she got political. I don't know. But she stopped. She gave the photos to that reporter Kresge and told him to sit on them. Then she cut a deal with Smith that we would sit tight with the dam so long as he and his cronies in the Senate wouldn't push for a new Compact. So *we* got half of Glen Canyon, and *he* got the other half. But half wasn't what we wanted. It wasn't what I wanted. I wanted it all."

"So you killed her and tried to do it yourself."

For a moment Josh looked as if he might cry. He pounded his hand on the steering wheel over and over again and punched the glass of the windshield of the Jeep, leaving a smear of blood. "That fucking bitch had it coming! I tried to talk sense into her. We even walked down the Hole in the Rock to look at what those fuckers had done to the Glen, but she said we had to be realistic."

"You executed her."

"We were camped at Dance Hall Rock. We argued all night. In the morning I put an end to the argument."

"Why did you dump her in Lake Powell?"

"She had to see what she'd done."

There was a very long silence. Robbie watched Hayduke out of the corner of his eye. After some time he asked, "And the others?"

"That was after. It was your father's fault. If he hadn't started snooping around they would still be alive. But he was getting too close with that Hopi girl he found back in Courthouse Wash. So I had to kill the others so they wouldn't start all working together."

"You led my dad right to you."

"I had to. I had to find out what he knew."

"The journal. That's how you did it. You knew that he would go to that kiva in Harris Wash after he learned that the Wisechild woman had been working there and you planted the journal for him to find. You tried to kill him when he was there."

"Fuck, man, I could have killed your old man a dozen times by then. I had already been in his place a few times. Once I was there and he came home. I was hiding under his bed. I left when he got into the shower. But yeah, I followed him into Harris Wash and when he went down into the kiva looking for whatever he was looking for, I untied the rope."

"Why not just shoot him like you did Penelope? Or knock him out with chloroform like you did me, Darcy, and Kiel?" Robbie was making a leap but it seemed to fit.

"I didn't want it to be obvious. I hadn't even done Darcy at that point. I thought if I could get Silas out of the picture, make it look like he just got stuck in that kiva and died there, then I could keep on trying to tear down the dam and leave it at that. But your old man, he's got a lot of fight in him."

"So now what?" The Jeep stopped. In the distance was another spire of stone.

"Now we wait." Hayduke got out of the Jeep, opened the door, and went around and pulled Robbie out. Robbie hit the ground like a sack of wet laundry. He managed to right himself.

"You know, you're not going to be able to escape into the Canyons. They'll find you. It's really not that remote. I bet you last a day, maybe two. And when they find you, you're going to find yourself on death row."

Josh struck him in the side of the face with the butt of his pistol. A thread of blood leaked from Robbie's cheek.

"You could plead out, call it insanity—"

Another sharp blow; this time Robbie fell on the ground and spit blood. Josh kicked him in the ribs and then the face. Robbie's world swam around him and then went black.

Josh stood up and holstered his weapon. He started the Jeep up and drove it down a narrow wash, between the outstretched arms of juniper trees. He took a duffel bag from the back of the vehicle, removed a camouflage net from the bag and draped it over the Jeep, and used a juniper branch to brush the tracks of the Jeep from the wash. He tossed the branch to the side of the road. He checked his watch. Another few hours and Silas should be coming along.

He drew in a deep breath and looked around at the circling sky and the distant canyon walls, bright in the afternoon sun. The story was almost over. He felt a tremendous relief.

48

SHE TOUCHED HIS FACE. HE was lying on the sand on his back, his arms outstretched as if he were Jesus Christ lost in supplication. He could hear the river close by. Always flowing, never the same river twice.

"But what is life? The bird that flies from the night into the lighted banquet hall circles twice around the blazing candles and then flies out." Her voice was soft, like a gentle breeze.

He forced himself to open his eyes. She was smiling at him. She touched his face.

Don't go.

"I have to. It's time."

Please don't go.

"Life is short, Silas. Abbey said it himself. The bird that flies from the night. That's us. It's so very short. It's time for you to let go. It's time for you to wake up."

I don't want to.

"It's time to let go."

49

IN THE PERFECT SILENCE OF the Canyonlands, Silas didn't hear the shot.

He had his eyes closed. Josh had the Magnum pressed to his forehead, the hammer at full cock, and then . . . nothing happened.

Silas heard a heavy thud and felt the ground move. He opened his eyes. Josh was not there. Robbie was conscious and kneeling, a wild look on his face. He was shaking his head side to side. Next to him, on the ground, was Josh Charleston, a hole in the side of his head as big as a fist, the contents of his skull trailing for a yard across the broken surface of the American desert.

IT TOOK NEARLY a minute: four men swarmed Silas and Robbie. Two of them carried high-powered sniper rifles, their long tan-colored barrels extended with heavy silencers. The others carried the weapon Katie had called a CAR-15. They were dressed head to foot in desert camouflage and all had helmets, face masks, and eye goggles on. One man quickly took the .357 Magnum from Josh's hand and lowered the hammer gently. He placed the weapon on a flat piece of red stone. Two men went to Robbie and unbound his wrists and mouth. The fourth attended to Silas.

The man who checked on Silas said, "Are you Dr. Pearson?" Silas nodded. The man pressed on his own throat. "Package secure. One target down. Land the bird."

Robbie stumbled into his father's arms. Silas wrapped him tightly there. "It's alright, son, it's over now."

They both looked down at the body on the sand and stone.

"Where's Katie? Is she alive?" asked Silas.

"We don't have Dr. Rain yet, sir."

Silas stood up quickly.

"Please, Dr. Pearson, we'll take care of this."

"I have to find her." He broke from the small circle of men. He could hear a helicopter in the distance. He ran in the direction that Hayduke had emerged from, toward the base of Standing Rock. On the far side he found her. "She's here! She's here!"

He crouched down. She was lying on her side, her head bleeding, a heavy stone beside her. Silas felt for a pulse; his own heart was racing so fast he couldn't tell if he felt her heartbeat or his own. He rolled her over and put his head to her chest and then near her mouth, listening for the intake of breath. The adrenaline in his system seemed to mask all of his senses.

He tilted her head back and was about to start CPR when she coughed once and opened her eyes.

"Oh, thank Christ," he said, sitting back and putting his head in his hands. "Thank God."

Rain coughed again as two of the FBI tactical unit members reached the top of the debris cone at the base of Standing Rock.

"Dr. Rain, are you alright?"

"I'm alright. Head hurts. Could use some water." She turned to Silas and said weakly, "If you wanted to kiss me, you could have just done it when I was awake."

A Little Bird helicopter emerged from the direction of the Orange Cliffs and set down on the road. Dwight Taylor and Eugene Nielsen emerged along with two other members of the FBI Hostage Rescue Team. Rain sat up and waved, and they waved back. The FBI team members gave Rain water and attended to the wound on the side of her head.

Silas stood and walked to the north, to where the plateau dropped off into the Maze and the dendritic branch canyons that led to Horse Canyon, the Green River, and then the Colorado.

Penelope was right, of course. It was time to say goodbye.

INSIDE OF AN hour there were a dozen law enforcement vehicles and a second, larger helicopter at Standing Rock. A sheriff's deputy from nearby Kane County was brought in to serve as the medical examiner for the case, and the sheriffs of Garfield and Wayne Counties attended the crime scene. FBI evidence recovery technicians Huston and Unger arrived by air from Monticello. A medical team attended to Silas, Robbie, and Katie.

Assistant Special Agent in Charge Dwight Taylor stood nearby as the EMT patched the various rents on the three friends' faces. Silas winced as a suture was sewn into his cheek. When the doctoring was done, he patted his son's knee and smiled at Katie Rain. "How? How did they find us?"

"I called Eugene before we left Escalante. I have a GPS tracking device in my truck. They were on us from the time we reached the White Canyon Bridge all the way. I used my government cell phone—the one you didn't crush with your boot—to call Dwight while I pretended to go for a pee. I'm sorry, Silas."

"I'm the one who should be sorry."

"I trusted Taylor's team."

"It saved all of our lives," said Silas, looking down and shaking his head. "As much as I'm glad this is all over, something is going to eat at me for some time to come. I'll never learn why. Why did Josh have to kill them?"

Robbie cleared his throat and looked from his father to Taylor and back. "I think I can help you with that."

50

THERE WAS SNOW ON THE ground. Underfoot the needles from juniper and pinion pine crunched, sending waves of autumnal scent into the cool fall air.

They parked at the Visitor Center on the South Rim of the Grand Canyon and, shunning the wide, paved path, stepped into the airy forest. Nobody said anything as they walked, back and forth, picking a route at random through the woods.

A black-winged, full-bodied raven sat at the top of a twisted juniper and croaked, his voice a harsh call, puffs of breath condensing as fog against a deep blue sky.

The three men paused, watched the bird a moment, and carried on.

All at once the space around them seemed to lighten; the thin glow of late afternoon seemed to gain buoyancy as the trees parted. They crossed another paved hiking trail—six inches of snow rested on it—and then the world dropped away before them.

Silas used his boots to push snow from a slab of limestone just a few feet from edge of the canyon. From his pack he pulled out a blanket and put it on the stone. His two sons stood slack-jawed, staring in amazement at the delicate pink hue of the stone that stretched for sixteen miles to the snow-clad North Rim.

"I promised Penny that I would take both of you here one day. She liked the way it felt to come upon the canyon as if it were a surprise; it was like discovering it over and over again."

The boys sat down next to their father. Robbie put a hand on his dad's arm. Silas pulled the journal from his pack, rested it on his lap, and patted it gently.

51

IN AN HOUR THE SUN would be down. Silas moved quickly up the trail, a few small patches of late spring snow accenting the brilliant red sandstone. The golden evening light seemed to get caught in the sandstone like leaves blown from cottonwood trees. The layers of stone looked like ripples on the ocean, frozen in time, painted red as if to accentuate the point.

There was no one else on the trail to the popular destination. In late March there were few tourists in Arches National Park, and any locals who were in the vicinity were likely already enjoying the world-famous view that Silas was rushing to take in. He was breathing hard and almost running up the trail.

Silas wore a wool cap, pulled down over his ears, and carried a light pack. If he'd spilled its contents on the ground even he would have been surprised. There was no GPS unit ticking off the miles of his five-year-long, lonesome search. There was no topo sheet, cross-hatched and colored to indicate the demarcation of his long hunt. No jumars, no length of nylon climbing rope, no frozen bottles of water.

The bottle of wine and plastic wine goblets would have seemed utterly foreign.

Ahead, on the crest of land that gave way to the amphitheatre, a figure was backlit. "Hurry up, old man," came a singsong voice.

Silas smiled. His face, often sunburnt and wind-blasted, seemed to have softened, taking a few years from his countenance. Even his porcupine-quill hair had grown back in softer after the previous fall's scorching. He was a new man, reborn.

He reached the top of the rise. The basin beyond was shaped like an oblong dish, with high-backed red walls on three sides and on the fourth an open portal that gave a tremendous view to the snow-capped, cloud-cloaked La Sal Mountains in the distance. In the foreground the familiar shape of massive and iconic Delicate Arch glowed in the final light of day.

"How did you get up here so fast?"

"It's not every day I get to out-hike the great Silas Pearson." Katie Rain smiled. She was decked out in a bright down coat to guard against the early spring chill.

"It might be. These legs aren't getting any younger."

"Come on, let's find a good seat."

They clambered down into the basin. There was one other person there, a photographer set up and shooting the setting sun. Out of respect they found a seat out of his line of sight and on the far side of the amphitheatre. Later in the spring there would be hundreds of people in this bowl watching the sun set every night. For now they had the place to themselves.

They sat down on a blanket that Katie pulled from her pack. Silas opened the wine. They leaned back against the sandstone and watched in silence for a while. From time to time one of them would point to some patch of light glowing on the distant mountains, or comment on the color of the rock in the basin. Otherwise they sat in silence. For once there was nothing else to say.

The sun sank below the curving earth and the show ended for another night. The photographer packed up and left. Katie and Silas remained, seated next to one another.

"I don't really know what to do with myself these days," Silas said quietly.

Katie said nothing. She touched his arm gently.

"I mean, I've got my little project. In fact, I forgot to tell you, but I got my first order of books in today. I don't even have the store finished, but I've got books. In about a week I'll be able to hang out the shingle for the new, improved Red Rock Canyon Bookstore."

"What does Mary at Back of Beyond think?"

"They've had Main Street all to themselves for, what, thirty years? Competition is the American way, or so I'm told. The store is fun, and it's going to be a good way to spend some time during the tourist season, but sometimes I wake up and I look at my bare walls, where there used to be nothing but maps, and I don't know what to do."

"What about travel? See the world?"

"I've been to Vancouver twice this winter. Does that count?"

"I'm sure it was lovely, but I was thinking more along the lines of Africa or India."

"Maybe. I'm just restless, that's all."

"It will pass, Silas. You've spent five years completely focused on a mission. You wore yourself out. Maybe having a little time to just kick about Moab and the Castle Valley isn't such a bad thing. If you get too bored, come up to Salt Lake and I'll show you around the lab. That will curl your toes."

"I might just do that."

The last light of the evening was seeping from the landscape. The glow of reds, oranges, and pale whites was eclipsed by the inchoate night, a palette of deep blues and grays and, in the parabola of heaven, a perfect blackness, pocked only by a few tentative stars. Silas pushed himself to standing and reached a hand down to help Katie up. She was smiling at him.

EPILOGUE

THEY STOOD ON SEPARATE SHORES. He on a sandbar where the Green and the Colorado Rivers met; she on the opposite bank, watching the waters merge to form one great river. Despite the distance and the thrum of the rapids downstream, he could hear her speak as if she was beside him.

"Now you understand," she said.

He nodded.

"It was always about this place."

"I wish I had come here with you."

"You still can."

He nodded, reaching up to push a tear from his eyes.

"You know that I always had one great love; all others came second."

"I know; this place is—"

"It was *you*, Silas. Everything else came second. I just got caught up in things."

"Penny, I miss you."

"When you come here, think of me, but don't dwell. Life's too short, too beautiful, too precious."

"I'm trying."

"There's still one more, Silas. You've found Darcy and Kiel, but Tabby is still missing."

"I wouldn't know where to start." He looked at the river curling before him, the sound of it, a gentle hiss where it pulled at the sand bank. He heard a raven overhead and when he looked up she was gone.

The words seemed to emanate from downstream, beyond Cataract Canyon, from the ghost of Glen Canyon. "For myself, I choose to listen to the river for awhile, thinking river thoughts, before joining the night and the stars."

"I HOPE IT'S not too early to call."

"I'm going to have to change my cell number, Dr. Pearson. But no, it's not too early. We haven't talked in what, six months?"

"Something like that. Listen, I wonder if you can tell me if you're making any progress on the Tabby Dingwall case."

"It's funny you should ask. I was just reviewing that file yesterday. We've reached a dead end. Why?" Dwight Taylor's voice dropped an octave. Silas thought he heard the skepticism there.

"I think I might be able to help you."

ACKNOWLEDGMENTS

There are, as always, many people to be grateful to for their help in writing this book. None more important than my wife Jenn, who puts up with me crawling out of bed at five every morning so I can find time to write, and who has joined me on my explorations of the canyon country as I first conceived, and then completed, this series.

Taryn Boyd at Touchwood Editions has taken a chance on Silas Pearson and for that I'm grateful. Pete Kohut continues to create covers and designs that exceed the content between the pages, and Cailey Cavallin helps make sense of that content with her editorial prowess. Frances Thorsen, my story editor, keeps me on the straight and narrow, not letting me get away with too much creative license.

Supervisory Special Agent Jonathan B. Zeitlan of the FBI's public affairs division was a tremendous resource throughout the development of this story. Stephanie Halmhofer, an osteoarchaeologist, has been critical to my research. Sheriff James D. Perkins Jr. of Garfield County, Utah, provided important insight into policing that vast, sparsely populated region.

I am particularly grateful to my hometown bookstore, Cafe Books of Canmore, Alberta. The support of a local bookseller is invaluable, not only for sales, but for moral support. The very real Back of Beyond Books in Moab, Utah, has been very kind in their support.

Darren and Devon from Moab's Tex's Riverways were part of the hive-mind that helped create this series, and have answered questions over the five years it took to pen these three novels. Thanks boys. Greer Chesher and Kim Crumbo have pitched in with great advice and research.

Finally, I am profoundly glad for the all the people who work to protect the landscapes and cultures of the American Southwest. In particular, my hat is off to the folks at the Southern Utah Wilderness Alliance and the Glen Canyon Institute for their tireless work in defense of this profoundly beautiful landscape. I am grateful for your diligence and determination.

And finally, my thanks to Edward Abbey. I never met him, and maybe that's for the best, but every one of his books inspired me; it was for him, and the landscape that he loved, that this series was written.

STEPHEN LEGAULT is an author, photographer, consultant, and conservation activist who lives in Canmore, Alberta. He is the author of ten other books, including *The Slickrock Paradox* and *Black Sun Descending*, the first two books in the Red Rock Canyon mystery series. Stephen has also penned four installments in the Cole Blackwater mystery series: *The Glacier Gallows*, *The Vanishing Track*, *The Cardinal Divide*, and *The Darkening Archipelago*, as well as *The End of the Line* and *The Third Riel Conspiracy*, the first two books in the Durrant Wallace mystery series. Please visit Stephen online at stephenlegault.com, connect with him on Facebook, or follow him on Twitter at @stephenlegault.

OTHER BOOKS BY STEPHEN LEGAULT

Carry Tiger to Mountain: The Tao of Activism and Leadership
Running Toward Stillness

THE DURRANT WALLACE SERIES
The End of the Line
The Third Riel Conspiracy

THE RED ROCK CANYON SERIES
The Slickrock Paradox
Black Sun Descending
The Same River Twice

THE COLE BLACKWATER SERIES
The Cardinal Divide
The Darkening Archipelago
The Vanishing Track
The Glacier Gallows